Rachel Renée Russell

D♥RK diaries

I Love Paris!

with Nikki Russell and Erin Russell

SIMON AND SCHUSTER

First published in Great Britain in 2023 by Simon & Schuster UK Ltd

First published in the USA in 2023 as *Dork Diaries: Tales from a Not-So-Posh Paris Adventure*, by Aladdin, an imprint of Simon & Schuster Children's Publishing Division, 1230 Avenue of the Americas, New York, New York 10020

1 3 5 7 9 10 8 6 4 2

Simon & Schuster UK Ltd
1st Floor, 222 Gray's Inn Road
London WC1X 8HB

www.simonandschuster.co.uk
www.simonandschuster.com.au
www.simonandschuster.co.in

Simon & Schuster Australia, Sydney
Simon & Schuster India, New Delhi

A CIP catalogue record for this book is available from the British Library.

HB ISBN 978-1-4711-9683-6
eBook ISBN 978-1-4711-9684-3
eAudio ISBN 978-1-3985-0108-9

Printed and Bound in the UK using 100% Renewable Electricity at CPI Group (UK) Ltd

MIX
Paper | Supporting responsible forestry
FSC® C171272

To Ca'marii Latrice,
Samantha Yessenia,
and
Sydney Renise

You are my favorite SUPERFANS.
Stay nice, smart, and DORKY!

FRIDAY, AUGUST 1

Well, it looks like my FIFTEEN MINUTES OF FAME are finally over ☹!

YES! It was a MIND-BLOWING experience to be the opening act for the BAD BOYZ, a world-famous BOY BAND! I was heartbroken (along with millions of their fans) when they ended their tour early to take a break.

Now I'm STUCK at home for the rest of the summer, and my life is pretty much back to normal. "Normal" meaning EXCRUCIATINGLY BORING! So, for a little excitement, my bandmates and I agreed to do a FREE concert tonight for our local Summer Fun Fest. Hey, the $100 gift cards they offered us from the CupCakery made it impossible to refuse ☺!

We were performing after Pickles the Juggling Clown and before my neighbor Mrs. Wallabanger and her FIERCE squad of elderly belly dancers. We're pros! Like, how hard could this GIG be?! . . .

1

OMG!
I COULD NOT
BELIEVE
THIS WAS
HAPPENING
TO ME ☹!!

Unfortunately, my FRENEMY, MacKenzie Hollister, has a really bad habit of popping up at the WORST POSSIBLE TIME! Like a huge, pus-filled ZIT that magically appears on the end of your NOSE.

On your way to SCHOOL!

On PICTURE DAY!!

I quickly pulled the curtain back over my head.

All I wanted to do right then was dig a really deep hole, crawl into it, and . . .

DIE!!

I HAD A COMPLETE MELTDOWN!

My WORST NIGHTMARE had come true!

Or . . . HAD IT?!!

Whenever I get SUPERstressed out about something, I ALWAYS have a bad dream about it.

Like the time I had a HORRIBLE nightmare about my BIRTHDAY PARTY! . . .

I DREAMED THAT MACKENZIE
"ACCIDENTALLY" PUSHED ME HEADFIRST
INTO MY BIRTHDAY CAKE!!

So it was VERY possible that my CHAOTIC CONCERT CATASTROPHE was ONLY a NIGHTMARE!

And any second now I was going to WAKE UP in my bedroom, drenched in a cold sweat, totally RELIEVED that it was ALL just a figment of my imagination.

PLEASE! PLEEASE!! PLEEEEASE!!!...

LET ALL OF THIS BE A REALLY. BAD. DREAM!!

!

17

SATURDAY, AUGUST 2

When I woke up this morning, I slowly opened my eyes.

The sun was shining, and the birds were chirping. OMG! I felt SO relieved ☺!

For TWO SECONDS.

Then the HORRIFIC memories of that concert came WHOOSHING back in a huge tidal wave, like someone had, um . . . FLUSHED a TOILET . . . inside my, um . . . BRAIN ☹!

Unfortunately, it WASN'T all just a bad dream.

I remember every single detail like it was yesterday.

WAIT! That WAS yesterday! Our concert was SURREAL.

I could NOT believe the stage curtain actually fell on us.

It was like we were suddenly covered by a humongous, freakishly dark CLOUD of, um . . .

I remember thinking the only GOOD thing about this very BAD situation was that it could NOT possibly get any WORSE!

But I was WRONG!! Things got A LOT worse.

Someone made a public announcement that our performance was "a TOTAL DISASTER"!

And then she actually wondered aloud if we'd "STILL get those cupcakes" as promised. Talk about

TOTAL HUMILIATION!

Like, WHO would even say such CRUEL and HEARTLESS things like that about CHILDREN?!

Well, okay. We're actually TEENS!! But STILL . . . !!

And when I cautiously peeked out from under the curtain, I totally FREAKED OUT!

MacKenzie Hollister was in the front row RECORDING the entire thing with her cell phone ☹!

And get this!!

She had the nerve to walk right up to me and shove her cell phone in my face (without my permission) like we were BFFs about to take a SELFIE or something!

Calling MacKenzie a MEAN GIRL is an understatement.

She's a SCORPION with blond hair extensions, designer shoes, and pink glittery eye shadow! . . .

20

MACKENZIE IS SUPERCUTE,
GLAM, AND DEADLY!!

I have no idea why that girl HATES my GUTS!!

Anyway, now MacKenzie has a PERMANENT
record of the most HUMILIATING

21

thing that has EVER happened to me!!

I'm SUCH a KLUTZ!

I totally deserve to be kicked out of the band for RUINING our show.

But my bandmates just said "Accidents happen" and "It wasn't a big deal."

I think they felt sorry for me and were just trying to make me feel better.

Hopefully, we'll STILL get those gift cards for cupcakes. My friends DEFINITELY earned them.

My BFFs, Chloe and Zoey, are supposed to meet me at the CupCakery tomorrow at 4:00 p.m. to pick them up.

But I'm SO embarrassed about what happened, I'm SERIOUSLY thinking about just HIDING OUT for the rest of the summer.

In my BEDROOM CLOSET! . . .

NOTE TO SELF: Remember to stock up on batteries for my flashlight ☺!

It has been two days since I publicly humiliated myself, and I'm STILL feeling down in the dumps. . . .

← ME

The LAST thing I wanted to do was hang out with Chloe and Zoey at the CupCakery.

So I texted my BFFs and gave them the lame excuse that I couldn't go because I was busy cleaning my room.

I was surprised when they actually volunteered to come over and help me. This made no sense WHATSOEVER because Chloe and Zoey were ALWAYS complaining about how much they HATED cleaning their OWN rooms!

WHY were they suddenly so ANXIOUS to help ME clean MINE?!!

Finally I gave in and agreed to meet them at the CupCakery. But then they insisted on picking me up.

And during the car ride over, I noticed they were acting very suspicious and texting each other even though they were both sitting in the back seat.

When I got to the CupCakery, I discovered why. . . .

ALL MY BANDMATES HAD COME
TO CHEER ME UP ☺!

OMG!

I suddenly felt SO overwhelmed with emotion, I thought I was going to break down and UGLY CRY right there in front of everyone!

Chloe, Zoey, Violet, Brandon, Theo, and Marc are the BEST. FRIENDS. EVER! We actually laughed about my accident.

Although none of us could figure out how that open bottle of water just mysteriously appeared on the stage.

We also talked about how in just FOUR WEEKS we were heading back to school again.

Our summer had been totally ruined by the Bad Boyz tour ending abruptly. But I felt we could STILL spend the next few weeks doing the FUN things we had sacrificed by going on tour.

That's when I came up with a BRILLIANT idea called the SAVAGE SUMMER CHALLENGE!

Each of us had to agree to try an exciting and challenging activity that we've always wanted to do but were too scared to actually try.

Everyone LOVED my idea! So we all decided to just GO FOR IT!!

Personally, I've always wanted to learn fashion illustration because I love that chic, gorgeous style of art. But I thought it would be way too difficult for me.

My friends felt exactly the same way about their goals.

Since we were discussing our challenges, I decided to share a personal struggle that I'd been having since our last concert. I explained how just the thought of performing onstage again was enough to give me a MASSIVE PANIC ATTACK!

I revealed that I was probably suffering from a very rare and debilitating PHOBIA called . . .

FOFOASAKDAC!

It's the medical abbreviation for the extreme
Fear Of Falling Off A Stage And Knocking Down
A Curtain.

Everyone was very SHOCKED to hear that news!
I explained that the WORST thing about it
was that I felt like the ENTIRE WORLD was
LAUGHING at ME!

But my friends ASSURED me that absolutely
NO ONE was laughing at me.

Except maybe MacKenzie.

But she DIDN'T really count because she LAUGHS
at EVERYBODY!

They told me not to worry and that I was probably
still stressed out and a little traumatized by
everything that had happened to me.

I had to admit, they were probably right.

Like, what sane and rational person would even care about what happened at some RANDOM, small-town Summer Fun Fest concert?!

OMG! Hanging out with my SUPERsupportive friends made me feel SO much better!

I'm really LUCKY to have them in my life!

By the time we left, I'd totally forgotten how AWFUL I'd been feeling for the past couple of days.

I was finally back to my normal,

HAPPY, ENERGETIC, and CONFIDENT self!

But then I realized I had left my gift card on the table and went back into the CupCakery to get it! . . .

I ACCIDENTALLY OVERHEAR KIDS FROM MY
SCHOOL TALKING TRASH ABOUT ME!

Some guy was pointing at MY FACE on HIS cell phone while he and his friends had uncontrollable fits of HYSTERICAL laughter.

CLOWN ACT?! SERIOUSLY, DUDE?!!

I just stood there, STARING at them in SHOCK.

What little dignity and self-respect I had left just SHRIVELED UP, CRAWLED AWAY, and DIED!!

OMG! I was RIGHT all along!

THE ENTIRE WORLD REALLY IS LAUGHING AT . . .

ME!!

☹!

MONDAY, AUGUST 4

The stuff I overheard those kids say about me was stuck in my head and playing on repeat.

It got so bad, I was seriously thinking about QUITTING my band. But after getting a good night's rest, I'm starting to have second thoughts.

I think Chloe and Zoey are probably right. I'm TOTALLY overreacting.

Accidents happen. It's NOT the end of the world.

I really LOVE performing with my band. Even if it means sharing the stage with Pickles the Clown and being paid with CUPCAKES.

Also, school starts in a few weeks, and by that time, kids won't remember any of this or even care.

I need to stop stressing out over every little thing and just CHILLAX!

My thoughts were interrupted when I heard Brianna outside in the hall blasting my song "DORKS RULE!"

She was singing so horribly off-key, I thought my ears were going to bleed!

But it made me smile! Hey, even my kid sister was a HUGE fan! I suddenly felt all warm and fuzzy!

I opened my bedroom door and peeked outside. I was NOT expecting to see Brianna and her wacky hand puppet, Miss Penelope, wearing MY expensive stage costume made by the famous fashion designer Blaine Blackwell!

"BRIANNA! PLEASE TAKE THAT OFF RIGHT NOW! IT'S NOT A TOY, AND YOU'RE GOING TO RUIN IT! YOU DID NOT ASK PERMISSION TO WEAR IT!"

Sometimes when I open my mouth, my mother comes out! It's actually kind of scary ☹!

Brianna's response made me feel like I had just been PUNCHED in the GUT. . . .

WAIT, NIKKI! I NEED TO GET TO THE FUNNY PART, WHEN I ALMOST FALL OFF THE STAGE!

MISS PENELOPE

BRIANNA, IMPERSONATING ME ☹!

She had attended the concert with my parents. But I had no idea my OWN little sister thought I was a TOTAL JOKE too!

I stared in disbelief as Brianna suddenly fell over and rolled down the hall with her arms flailing.

She ended her song sprawled out on the floor with a ~~curtain~~ blanket over her head.

I hate to admit it, but her impression of me was spot-on and HILARIOUS ☺!

But STILL . . . ☹!!

"Nikki, you were FUNNIER than Pickles the Clown!" Brianna giggled. "Miss Penelope thinks so too!"

Looking back, I was probably a little harsh.

I made Brianna take off my costume. Then I gave her a stern lecture about respecting the property of others that ended with a not-so-subtle threat. . . .

ME, CANCELING BRIANNA'S LITTLE CONCERT!

Next I gathered up all my stuff and put it exactly where it quite obviously belonged. . . .

37

. . . IN THE GARBAGE BIN!

I guess MacKenzie was RIGHT!

My music career is SO over!!

☹!!

Today I stayed in bed for hours just STARING at the wall and SULKING ☹! For some reason it always makes me feel better ☺!

My mom came into my room around noon to make sure I was still alive. She even checked my forehead to see if I had a fever.

I pretended to be asleep so she'd go away. The last thing I needed was my mom CRASHING my PERSONAL PITY PARTY!

I was STILL upset about that conversation I overheard at the CupCakery.

If those kids saw the HUMILIATING video of me on SOCIAL MEDIA, that meant the entire WORLD had probably seen it!

And, unfortunately, the entire WORLD includes . . . ALL THE STUDENTS AT MY SCHOOL!!

ME, TOTALLY FREAKING OUT
THAT I'M ALREADY A HUMONGOUS
JOKE ON SOCIAL MEDIA EVEN BEFORE
THE SCHOOL YEAR HAS STARTED!!

How PATHETIC is that?!

It's one thing for ME to ruin MY life!

But NO WAY am I going to RUIN the lives of my FRIENDS.

The first thing I need to do is QUIT my BAND!

As much as I hate to do this, I don't have a choice.

I'm SUCH an EMBARRASSMENT!!

I'll just send everyone an honest, heartfelt letter explaining my decision and hope they'll understand.

However, instead of writing SIX letters, I decided to create a form letter that I could easily personalize for each of my bandmates:

MY BAND RESIGNATION FORM LETTER

Dear _____,

    A. Chloe   D. Violet

    B. Zoey   E. Marcus

    C. Brandon   F. Theodore

I realize you are probably very:

    A. thrilled   C. mystified

    B. ticked   D. shook

to be receiving this unexpected letter.

But after a lot of:

A. soul-searching   C. bad hair days

B. cheese fries   D. toenail fungus

I have made the very difficult decision that it would be best for me to leave our band.

I will NEVER, EVER forget all the wonderful times we shared together:

A. sweating like pigs under hot stage lights

B. feeling so nervous we thought we were going to throw up our lunches

C. forgetting the lyrics to our songs

D. practically FALLING OFF the stage

in front of THOUSANDS of adoring fans
clutching homemade signs and screaming
our names.

Since you will be needing a new lead
singer, I think you should definitely NOT
consider:

A. Brianna, THE delusional expert to
the stars.

B. Mrs. Wallabanger and her squad of
elderly belly dancers.

C. Pickles the Juggling Clown.

D. MacKenzie, the glamorous SCORPION
in lip gloss.

I cannot begin to express how much
I have cherished our totally AWESOME
friendship. You will FOREVER be in my

heart, and I'm REALLY going to miss you. Best of luck in the future!

Your friend,
Nikki Maxwell

OMG! This letter is so SAD!

I can't stop CRYING!!

☹!

OMG! Things are even WORSE than I imagined. I knew I was being LAUGHED at by kids in high school and middle school. But I had no idea that ELEMENTARY SCHOOL kids were LAUGHING at me too ☹!!

Brianna's friends were already BEGGING her to take ME to school for SHOW-AND-TELL in the fall!

Lately, I've been seriously thinking about transferring to a NEW SCHOOL.

AGAIN!

It should be far enough away that students haven't SEEN the video or HEARD all the gossip about my little "accident."

I personally think the PERFECT school would be located a bit farther away from home. You know, in a place like . . .

SIBERIA.

Anyway, I've FINALLY made up my mind! I'm going to e-mail those letters to my friends right now to let them know I'm leaving the band and won't be hanging out with them at school anymore.

You know, due to the whole SIBERIA thing!

JUST GREAT ☹! My cell phone is ringing, and it's—

OMG!!!...

I CAN'T believe WHO is calling me right now ☺!!

I'll finish this diary entry AFTER I take this call. Be right back!!

47

Okay, I'm back. I just got some FANTASTIC NEWS!
But I can't tell anyone yet! So . . .

I HAVE THE BIGGEST SECRET EVER!!!

SQUEEEEEEEEEEEE ☺!!

I CAN'T talk about it! Not even in my diary.

I'm literally DYING to tell SOMEONE!

ANYONE!!

But TREVOR CHASE, the famous music producer who works with all the biggest pop stars, including THE BAD BOYZ, warned me that everything we discussed on the phone is highly confidential.

He said that if I so much as breathe a single word of it, everything will be TOTALLY RUINED.

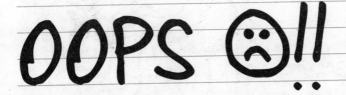

OOPS ☹!!

I've probably ALREADY said TOO MUCH!!

I'd better STOP writing NOW before I accidentally BLAB the big SECRET!

☹!!

My BFFs, Chloe and Zoey, have called me a half dozen times since yesterday.

And my crush, Brandon, has been blowing up my phone because I volunteered to help him out at Fuzzy Friends Animal Rescue Center.

But I haven't answered or returned ANY of their calls.

I'm totally GHOSTING my friends right now, and I feel HORRIBLE! But I don't have a choice.

I'm really worried I'll accidentally tell them the BIG SECRET and RUIN everything.

Obviously, I can't AVOID them FOREVER!

The next time I hang out with them, I'll just need to take subtle yet effective precautions to keep me from . . .

SPILLING MY GUTS!

Like, I can pretend to be wrapping a gift and . . .

. . . TAPE MY MOUTH SHUT!!

Everyone knows I'm a MESSY gift wrapper.

Or I could try . . .

. . . ZIPPING MY LIPS!!

I'll just tell everyone it's a trendy new chunky lip gloss flavor called PLEASE. SHUT. UP!

I could stuff my face with PIZZA and only talk with my mouth full. Then, even if I DID tell the secret, no one would understand a word I'd said. . . .

ME, STUFFING MY FACE WITH PIZZA!

Keeping such a HUMONGOUS secret from my BFFs, Chloe and Zoey, and Brandon is going to be . . .

PURE. UNADULTERATED. TORTURE!

But if necessary I'll take this SECRET to my GRAVE!! . . .

NIKKI
MAXWELL

BELOVED DAUGHTER
AND ADORED
SISTER . . .

WHO NEVER
BLABBED
THE BIG SECRET!!

MY HEADSTONE!!

I'm DEAD serious! No pun intended.

I need to stop stressing and just CHILLAX!!

I'VE GOT THIS! ☺!!

AAAAAAAHHHHHHH!!
That was me, SCREAMING in frustration!!

Trying to keep this secret is KILLING ME!!
I know Trevor said I couldn't TELL anyone.
But he NEVER said I couldn't WRITE about it
in my DIARY! Right?!

So that's exactly what I'm going to do ☺!

Or maybe NOT ☹!

But WHO is going to know? Unless there are, like . . .
people, um . . . SECRETLY READING . . . my diary!!

Last month my band was the opening act for the Bad
Boyz on the U.S. part of their world tour. Well . . .
until they nearly had a complete MELTDOWN!

They were SUPERstressed, burned out, and
squabbling with each other because they'd been on
tour continuously for the past YEAR.

Aidan Carpenter and Nicolas Perez are sixteen years old, and Victor Chen and Joshua Johnson are seventeen.

Most guys their age spend the summer working part-time jobs, hanging out with friends, shooting hoops, and playing video games. But these poor dudes were up at 5:00 a.m. on a grueling schedule packed with meetings, photo shoots, rehearsals, interviews, sound checks, and cross-country flights on private jets.

Finally, at the end of the day, when they were totally EXHAUSTED and ready to CRASH, they had to pull off the most DIFFICULT task of all: an intense, high-energy, two-hour concert in a huge arena jam-packed with thirty thousand SCREAMING FANS!!

Then . . . WASH, RINSE, and REPEAT!!

But get this! Trevor Chase called me two days ago with an exciting update. He told me the guys are enjoying their vacation and resting up to resume their world tour in the fall.

He admitted that things had gotten so bad, they were on the verge of breaking up and insisted that I had saved the band simply by convincing them to take some time off.

"We want to do something special for YOU and YOUR band to show our gratitude. Hey, after we abruptly ended the tour and ruined your summer, it's the least we can do!" Trevor joked.

Ruining my SUMMER was an understatement.

After humiliating myself at that Bummer-Summer Freaky-Fest, it felt like my entire LIFE was ruined! But I was NOT about to bring up ANY of that.

"Allowing us to open for the Bad Boyz was a once-in-a-lifetime opportunity and an awesome experience!" I gushed. "You don't need to do anything more."

I was just happy the Boyz DIDN'T break up.

Touring with them still feels like a DREAM! . . .

58

Trevor continued. "Actually, Nikki, we have an exciting project for you if you're interested. It includes an all-expenses-paid trip in about ten days! The Boyz are scheduled to be on location for a photo shoot for the cover of a magazine. But since they're taking a break, we thought YOUR band would be PERFECT. It'll be great exposure for you. I just need to get the editor of the magazine on board with the change in plans."

OMG! I almost fainted when I heard his offer!

Was it Los Angeles, New York, Miami, Chicago . . . ?!

Since Trevor was still working out the details, he WARNED me that I can't tell anyone, not even my bandmates, until everything is finalized.

My job is to keep my BIG MOUTH SHUT and to make sure everyone is available for the trip. But I haven't even gotten to the BEST part yet!

We'll be traveling to one of the most MAGNIFICENT cities in the ENTIRE world!! . . .

THE CITY OF LIGHT!!

Can you imagine ME on VACAY in PARIS?!!

SQUEEEEEEEEEEEE ☺!!!

~~OMG!!! I really need to start practicing my French!~~

OOH LA LA!!! J'ai vraiment besoin de commencer à pratiquer mon français!

I'll definitely need to be able to say these SUPERimportant phrases in French:

"Where is the Eiffel Tower?"

"How far is the Louvre Museum from here?"

"I would like five more of those yummy chocolate croissants, please!"

"Excuse me! But where can I buy one of those cool black berets that all the *très chic* French people wear?"

"I think I might be lost! Can you help me?"

"Where is the nearest bathroom? QUICK!"

"May I have fries with that?"

"Can you tell me where the Miraculous Ladybug girl lives?"

SQUEEEEEEEEEEE ☺!!

Hopefully, Trevor will figure out all the details and confirm everything ASAP!

In the meantime, I just need to do FOUR very SIMPLE things:

1. Keep this HUGE, AWESOME, and EXCITING SECRET for just a few more days.

2. Make sure my bandmates are available.

3. Start PACKING for PARIS.

4. Translate the French words I'll be using in my diary to English (see pages 321 to 323).

Like, how HARD can THIS be?!! ☺!!

I've been staring at my cell phone all morning, waiting impatiently for Trevor to call me back about our trip to Paris.

It's been THREE whole days since we last spoke! Which, under the circumstances, is practically like . . .

FOREVER!!

Maybe he changed his mind and offered the magazine cover to someone else. You know, a person a little more popular than we are.

Like . . . BEYONCÉ!

But here's what really worries me.

What if Trevor somehow found out about our Summer Fun Fest disaster?!

Thanks to MacKenzie, that video is plastered all over social media.

By now MILLIONS of people have probably
seen it!

WHO am I kidding?!

We're probably the LAST people some RITZY
French magazine would want to feature.

The ONLY magazine that would seriously consider
ME for the cover is . . .

CLOWNS-R-US ☹!

HOPEFULLY, I'll hear from Trevor soon.

And, in the meantime, I need to make sure my
bandmates are available to make this trip.

But . . . HOW?!

I can't just call them up every single day and
demand to know what their plans are.

That would be WAY too obvious. And WEIRD!

64

The ONLY way to find out everyone's personal BIZ is to SNOOP!! So I've been reading their social media and getting inside information from their family and friends.

WARNING! MOMS are NOTORIOUS for oversharing embarrassing photos of their children.

Posting an ancient potty-training photo on Facebook with five heart emojis and labeling it . . .

"POOPY CUTIE"

is not only HUMILIATING to us TEENS but should be considered CYBERBULLYING and punishable by one year in jail and a $5,000 fine!

We LOVE you, Mom! But YOU do the CRIME, YOU do the TIME!

Thank goodness no one under forty uses Facebook!

I really want this trip to Paris, and NOTHING is going to get in my way! So say GOOD-BYE to Nikki the dorky middle schooler, and HELLO to . . .

NICOLE J. MAXWELL,
SECRET SPY EXTRAORDINAIRE!

Here are my SPY ACTIVITY NOTES for today:
Chloe is taking cooking lessons from her grandma! . . .

World's Best Abuela

SAVAGE SUMMER!: COOKING LESSONS WITH GRANDMA

Today they baked double chocolate chip cookies.

Chloe literally lost her MIND over these cookies!
They were the reason we had that huge MIX-UP
and DRAMA with my birthday party invitations!

Chloe and her grandma are perfecting their cookie
recipe to enter a baking contest in two weeks.

Marc is an avid biker and has always wanted to compete in motocross. Well, today he did it! . . .

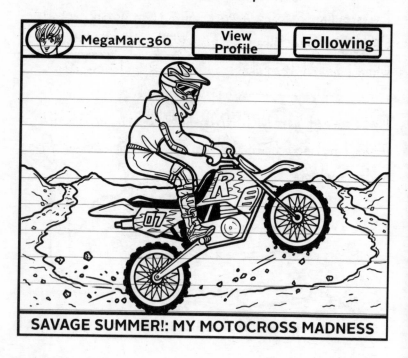

MegaMarc360   View Profile   Following

SAVAGE SUMMER!: MY MOTOCROSS MADNESS

If he does well in his next competition, he could qualify for regionals later this month.

Chloe and Marc are very busy, but hopefully NOT too busy for our trip to Paris. I'll need more intel.

Am I NOT a GENIUS at this ESPIONAGE stuff?! ☺!!

I was online reading a post on a teen gossip website ("Are the Bad Boyz REALLY Breaking Up?!!") when I heard footsteps outside my bedroom door.

I was sure it was BRIANNA sneaking around AGAIN ☹! Then I noticed that she had slipped a piece of paper under my door.

I had a hard time reading Brianna's sloppy handwriting, but it appeared to be a ticket of some kind:

I had just been invited to a magic show by
THE AMAZING BRIANNA-DINI.

LUCKY ME ☹!

Brianna is trying to earn yet another merit badge
in scouting, this time in MAGIC. She said it'll
be an important skill to have when she moves to
Baby Unicorn Island and starts working for Princess
Sugar Plum as an ASSISTANT MAGIC USER.

Brianna had borrowed a magic set from her
best friend, Oliver. And after just a few hours
of practice, she felt she was ready to share her
AWESOME magic skills with the world.

I decided to go along and pay the $1.00 fee for a
ticket even though it was a total RIP-OFF.

I was stuck babysitting since my parents were out.
So as long as she was playing quietly, I was happy!
Hey, when Brianna was bored, she could EASILY do
$1,000 worth of damage just to the stuff in my
bedroom!

70

When I arrived to her show, she gave me a special seat in the VIP section with her favorite toys. . . .

ME, SITTING IN THE
VERY IMPORTANT TOY SECTION

Then Brianna blew a kiss to her audience and quickly DISAPPEARED into her closet. At first I thought THAT was her magic act and the show was OVER ☹!

I was pretty disgusted I'd actually paid a whole dollar for an event that had lasted less than thirty seconds.

I was seriously thinking about contacting her management to demand a REFUND!

But then Brianna reemerged from the closet wearing a magician costume, complete with a top hat. She announced in a booming voice:

"LADIES AND GENTLEMEN! TOYS AND GIRLS! PLEASE WELCOME THE GREAT, THE AWESOME, THE FABULOUS . . . BRIANNA THE MAGICIAN! ALSO KNOWN AROUND THE WORLD AS . . . THE AMAAAAAZING BRIANNA-DINI!"

Brianna bowed and tipped her hat to the audience.

Then she pulled a big pink powder-puff thingy out of her pocket.

I was pretty sure it was the new one Mom had recently purchased to apply her makeup.

But now it was completely covered in baby powder.

"Prepare to be AMAAAAAZED!" the Amazing Brianna-dini bellowed as she slapped the powder puff and created a huge cloud of dust.

I had to admit, it almost looked like magical smoke or something.

I was EXTREMELY impressed!

UNLIKE how my parents were going to be when THEY got home. WHY?

Brianna's magician costume looked a lot like the fancy tuxedo and top hat Dad had RENTED to be the best man in his cousin's WEDDING next week.

Did I mention that his tux ALSO "magically" turned from shiny black to powdery white in an instant?

Dad was NOT going to be happy when MONEY "magically" disappeared from his WALLET due to his HUGE dry-cleaning bill.

"Thank you! Thank you!" the Amazing Brianna-dini said as she bowed again. "For my next trick, I will choose a person from the audience and saw 'em in half!" she announced. "Do I have any volunteers?"

SORRY!

But there was just NO WAY I was volunteering for THAT magic trick.

Especially for a BEGINNER magician who had only been doing magic for, like, TWO HOURS!

Brianna pointed to a cute fashion doll in a pink dress that was sitting near me.

"How about YOU, young lady?" she asked. Hey, better HER than ME!

The audience politely clapped for the very brave young lady.

This is what happened next. . . .

I was shocked and surprised to see Brianna with a small saw. I thought for sure she was going to use plastic props in her magic show.

"Brianna! Put that thing down!" I yelled at her. "There's no way I'm letting you use a real saw! Don't you know that it's dangerous to play with tools like that?"

"Don't worry, miss!" she said, and began sawing quickly. "I'm the AMAAAAAZING BRIANNA-DINI!"

Okay, I was starting to have a really BAD feeling about the AMAAAAAZING BRIANNA-DINI. She didn't even bother to wash her germy hands or sanitize that dirty saw before using it to do major surgery on that poor unsuspecting fashion doll. I couldn't bear to watch and covered my eyes!

Great news! I just got some new social media updates on my cell phone.

So I'll finish this WACKY story about Brianna's little "magic show" later!

Here are my SPY ACTIVITY NOTES for today:
Zoey started an online music vlog. . . .

SAVAGE SUMMER!: LOVING MY NEW MUSIC VLOG

It's called *Zoey Talks Music!* She shares her fave
songs with listeners and reviews popular tunes. She
also interviews up-and-coming teen musicians after
they perform live on her show.

Today she announced that she'll be covering the
Lollapalooza music festival in Chicago for several
days in August.

Theo recently joined a 3-on-3 street basketball league, and yesterday his team won! . . .

| TheoSwag35 | View Profile | Following |

SAVAGE SUMMER!: WE WON OUR FIRST 3X3 GAME

If Theo's team continues to win, they could qualify for semifinals, and ultimately finals.

OMG!! What if BOTH Zoey and Theo are out of town in August?!! Neither of them will be available to make the trip to Paris!

JUST GREAT ☹!!!

When we left the AMAZING BRIANNA-DINI, she was in the process of sawing her lovely volunteer in half.

I scrambled to my feet and ran up to the stage.

"BRIANNA! Give me that SAW! NOW!" I demanded.

"Here! Take it!" she said smugly as she handed it over. "I'm already done with it."

I took it from her, placed it safely back in Dad's toolbox in the garage, and returned to my seat.

"TA-DAAA!!!" Brianna sang as she showed off the shoebox that had been sawed in half.

"NOW! Watch as the AMAAAAAZING Brianna-dini uses her awesome magical powers to put this box and our lovely volunteer back together again!"

OH, REALLY?!! Now, THIS was a trick I was DYING to see!

Brianna slid the two halves of the box together, tapped them with her magic wand, and chanted:

"ALA-KAZOO! ALA-KAZAM!

UNICORN BOOGERS!

GREEN EGGS AND HAM!"

Then she hit the box really hard with the powder-puff thingy.

Baby powder went EVERYWHERE! Including, unfortunately, up my NOSE. I "magically" sneezed, like, seven times in a row.

"EWW! My tongue tastes like a BABY!" Brianna gagged as she fanned the powdery cloud away.

After dusting off her face, Brianna plastered on a huge smile and took another bow.

"Ladies and gentlemen! Now our lovely volunteer is magically back in one piece! TA-DAAA!!

Please, let's all give this brave young lady a round of applause!" The magician smiled.

I clapped loudly as I shook my head in disbelief.

OMG!

The AMAZING BRIANNA-DINI really WAS an amazing magician!

"Are you okay in there?" Brianna asked her lovely volunteer as she cautiously lifted a corner of the lid and peeked inside.

Suddenly Brianna's eyes got as big as saucers. She gasped and slammed the lid back down.

BAM!!

The entire audience was transfixed. It was so quiet in the room, you could hear a pin drop.

Then the Amazing Brianna-dini slowly separated the box, stared at it, and muttered . . .

I could see Brianna was starting to squirm.

"NIKKI, MY DOLL IS STILL SAWED IN HALF!" she whined loudly.

"That's EXACTLY why little kids SHOULD NOT play with TOOLS," I scolded her.

"But my MAGIC was supposed to FIX her!"

"Well, it DIDN'T! So, what do you have to say for yourself?" I asked, hoping she'd learned a lesson.

That's when Brianna just shrugged her shoulders and SMIRKED. . . .

Okay, NOW I was REALLY irritated!

"Brianna, this show is OVER! Now clean up this powdery mess before Mom and Dad get home!"

"But, Nikki, I'm not DONE yet! I need to pick ANOTHER lovely volunteer from the audience! The last one was, um . . . DEFECTIVE!"

"Brianna, YOUR MAGIC is DEFECTIVE! You are NOT going to SAW any more of your TOYS in HALF!" I yelled.

"That's NOT FAIR!" she screamed at me. "I need to practice my MAGIC so I can earn my scouting badge and work for Princess Sugar Plum!"

"Sorry! But you need to pick a new career. Now put away these toys and start cleaning up this mess. I need to go get the vacuum cleaner so I can vacuum Dad's tux and HIDE IT in the back of his CLOSET!"
I yelled at my bratty sister.

THANK GOODNESS
I didn't agree to be Brianna's lovely volunteer, or I'd be in the hospital EMERGENCY ROOM right now. . . .

ME, FREAKING OUT IN THE
EMERGENCY ROOM AFTER BRIANNA
PERFORMED HER MAGIC TRICK ON ME!!

But that's not even the SCARY part!

What if Brianna convinces her SCOUT TROOP LEADER to be her lovely volunteer in one of her magic shows?!

Brianna will SAW the poor woman in HALF and WON'T be able to put her back together again!!

After that little STUNT, she'll totally FAIL all four of the very important badge requirements: Ability to Perform Magic, Showmanship, Interacts Well with Audience, and Safely Uses Sharp Cutting Tools.

My little sister will NEVER earn that scouting badge in MAGIC or land her DREAM JOB with Princess Sugar Plum!

I couldn't help but feel SORRY for her. It looks like her situation is HOPELESS ☹!!

Anyway, I just got some new social media updates. Time to SNOOP again!

Here are my SPY ACTIVITY NOTES for today:
WOW! Brandon is giving FREE drum lessons . . .

SAVAGE SUMMER!: TEACHING DRUM LESSONS

. . . to little kids! So far he has four students,
including the CUTIE in this photo.

It's awesome that Brandon is volunteering for this
AND Fuzzy Friends. He's kind, caring, and has a
HUMONGOUS heart!

That's THREE reasons why he's my CRUSH ☺!

Violet recently joined a para dance sport team called THRILLS ON WHEELS ☺! . . .

VioletIsMy FaveColor   View Profile   Following

SAVAGE SUMMER!: LEARNING NEW DANCE ROUTINE

VERY COOL! She's practicing for a show at the mall and a competition in two weeks. It looks like Violet and Brandon are SUPERbusy in August too.

I think my espionage mission has been successfully completed! After several intense days of secretly SPYING on my friends, I have learned a slightly shocking yet indisputable FACT. . . .

My SAVAGE SUMMER CHALLENGE
was the . . .

WORST!

IDEA!!

EVER!!!

IT'S VERY POSSIBLE THAT NONE OF MY BANDMATES WILL BE AVAILABLE TO MAKE THAT TRIP TO PARIS!

AND IT'S ALL MY FAULT!!

Okay, I'm a little CONFUSED right now!

I just got a WEIRD text from Chloe and Zoey! . . .

CHLOE | ZOEY

Awesome news! Nikki, we have a big surprise just for YOU! Can't wait 2 tell U the details! R U at home right now?

I really don't LIKE surprises! Especially from Chloe and Zoey.

I know my BFFs mean well. But sometimes their

SMALL, very poorly planned SURPRISES accidentally turn into HUGE, unplanned DISASTERS!

I know I probably sound OVERDRAMATIC!

But my job is to make sure that NOTHING gets in the way of our trip to Paris!

And dealing with an unexpected "surprise" from Chloe and Zoey right now is a HUGE. RED. FLAG!

Soon the doorbell rang, and my BFFs rushed inside.

"Nikki, everyone is doing your Savage Summer Challenge and loving it!" Chloe exclaimed. "It was a BRILLIANT idea!"

"You challenged all of us to really push ourselves to accomplish something we've always dreamed about. We took your advice, and now we're KILLIN' IT! So, to show you how much we care, WE have a big surprise for YOU!" Zoey explained excitedly.

They both gave me a big hug and then said . . .

NIKKI, THANKS TO YOU, WE'RE ALL HAVING THE BEST SUMMER EVER! AND WE WANT YOU TO HAVE ONE TOO!

SO WE SIGNED YOU UP FOR ART CAMP! YOU LEAVE ON SATURDAY!

ISN'T THAT AWESOME?!!

MY BFFs TELL ME THEIR SURPRISE!!

"You said you always wanted to try fashion illustration, right? Well, going to art camp for two weeks will help you develop the confidence and the skillz to do it!" Zoey smiled.

"Nikki, you're the BEST FRIEND EVER!!" Chloe gushed. "You SO deserve this. And there's more. We signed you up to be a camp counselor, so art camp is TOTALLY FREE!! You just have to let them know if you want to come or not. If you decide to go, you leave in four days, on Saturday!"

"W-WAIT A MINUTE!! I'M SUPPOSED TO LEAVE ON S-SATURDAY?! FOR T-TWO WEEKS?!" I stammered in shock.

"Well, if you don't want to wait until Saturday, we can always ask if you can move in a few days EARLY!" Zoey offered.

"Nikki! WHY don't you move in . . . TOMORROW?!" Chloe squealed.

My BFFs excitedly raved about camp. But all I heard was "BLAH-BLAH, BLAH-BLAH, BLAH!" For a moment I seriously thought . . .

... MY HEAD WAS GOING TO EXPLODE!

ME, IN SHOCK ABOUT CHLOE
AND ZOEY'S BIG SURPRISE!

JUST GREAT ☹!

My summer is quickly turning into an even bigger DISASTER than it already was!!

All my band members are so BUSY with their personal Savage Summer Challenge projects that our trip to Paris is in jeopardy.

And NOW I'm scheduled to pack up and go to some CAMP for two weeks?!

Okay, I'll admit art camp actually sounds fun.

I'd been planning to go to one this summer until we got the opportunity to open for the Bad Boyz on tour.

"Nikki, I sincerely believe that art camp is going to change your LIFE!" Chloe gushed.

Then they insisted that we call the camp director so she could answer all our very important QUESTIONS, like . . .

ME, WITH MY BFFS, PRETENDING
TO BE SUPERexCITED ABOUT
GOING TO ART CAMP!!

After we finished our phone call, Chloe and Zoey left my house and headed home.

However, they had barely been gone ten minutes when I got another text message from them.

They were PESTERING me to stock up on a hefty supply of marshmallows (for s'mores), toilet paper, and bug spray for camp.

But I STILL have some UNANSWERED questions.

About PARIS, not ART CAMP!

It has been almost an entire week, and I STILL haven't heard anything from Trevor yet.

So I'm starting to get really worried.

WHY hasn't he called me back?! UNLESS . . . ?!

OMG! What if Trevor has seen a PHOTO, or worse yet, a VIDEO of our concert CATASTROPHE on social media?!

I have to be honest and ask myself a very difficult question.

Would Trevor Chase, the manager of the world-famous BAD BOYZ, risk RUINING HIS REP by doing a major project with THESE people?! . . .

NO WAY!!

We are, like . . . SO FIRED!!

I have a bad feeling that we are NEVER, EVER going to make that trip to PARIS!

I guess I'd better take my BFFs' advice and buy a truckload of MARSHMALLOWS, TOILET PAPER, and BUG SPRAY for camp.

☹!

WEDNESDAY, AUGUST 13

Brianna has been getting on my LAST NERVE!

The little brat is nagging me for autographs! She says she plans to sell them to the kids at her school and use the money to buy more tricks for her magic show and a baby unicorn.

After Mom and Dad left the house to run a few errands, I was shocked to see that Brianna was wearing her magician costume again!

Thank goodness she wasn't doing another of her magic shows that involved MUTILATING her toys.

I've been in a very FOUL mood ever since Chloe and Zoey decided to just SHIP me off to art camp! So today I didn't have the patience to deal with Brianna's crazy shenanigans.

However, I had a sneaking suspicion Brianna was secretly trying to HYPNOTIZE me with her Princess Sugar Plum heart necklace. . . .

ME, IN A VERY FOUL MOOD,
GLARING AT BRIANNA

Brianna was swinging it right in front of my face, back and forth and back and forth and back and forth, trying to hypnotize me into giving her autographs against my will.

Like, WHO does that?!!

"Brianna, you're wasting your time! Your silly magic is NOT working! Sorry, but I've already made up my mind, and my answer is still . . . YES, I WANT TO GIVE YOU MY AUTOGRAPH! I WANT TO GIVE YOU MY AUTOGRAPH!" I suddenly muttered in a trancelike state.

OMG! Brianna WAS actually HYPNOTIZING me!!

I was totally DISGUSTED and highly IMPRESSED at the same time!

"BRIANNA! STOP IT!" I scolded her, and snatched that necklace out of her hand.

I could NOT believe my own little sister would stoop SO low. Sorry, but kids today have NO integrity!

102

When Brianna heard our parents at the front door, she froze. Then, in a panic, she mysteriously DISAPPEARED into thin air. Like . . .

POOF!! I think she should add THAT little trick to her magic show. It's definitely my FAVE!

My mom told me to make a list of the things I needed for art camp, and we'd pick them up from the store. My list was pretty short. . . .

My Grocery List for CAMP

MARSHMALLOWS—A LOT

TOILET PAPER—A LOT

BUG SPRAY—A LOT

Once we got to the grocery store, my mom and I each grabbed a shopping cart and agreed to meet at the checkout lanes in fifteen minutes. . . .

I was grabbing stuff for camp when my cell phone suddenly rang. I was sure it was my mom checking in with me. But I was WRONG! . . .

ME, FREAKING OUT ABOUT THE CALL!

It was . . .

TREVOR CHASE!!

I almost dropped my phone as my heart started to pound. "Um . . . hello?" I said nervously.

"Nikki! Trevor here. I apologize for the delay, but I finally have an update on that trip to Paris. Are you available to talk right now?"

Actually, I was standing in the TOILET PAPER aisle of my local grocery store, and there was no PRIVACY whatsoever. Anyone could overhear us.

I was also a little DISTRACTED since I was walking, talking on the phone, shopping, and pushing the cart ALL at the same time.

But I'd been waiting for Trevor's call, like, FOREVER, and I was DYING to know if we were going to Paris. So I just took a deep breath and very calmly answered. . . .

I COULDN'T BELIEVE WHAT HAPPENED NEXT! ...

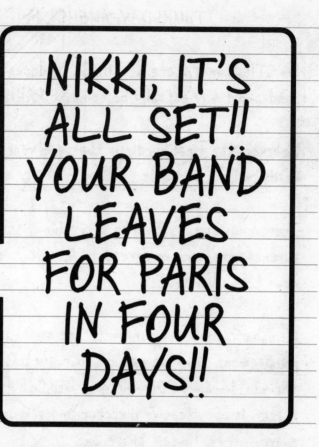

OMG! I did my Snoopy "happy dance" and tossed toilet paper streamers while people stared at me.

Then I yelled, "CLEANUP IN AISLE SEVEN, PLEASE!"

I'm STILL in a state of SHOCK. It looks like my band and I may actually be going to PARIS ☺!

However, the final hurdle is that everyone must be ready, willing, and able.

Trevor has already cleared everything with our parents. And they've agreed to let ME break the news to my bandmates.

We'll basically be working with the same Bad Boyz management team we had on tour. Victoria Steel, the world-famous Olympic gold medalist figure skater, is our creative director and personal prison guard . . . er, I mean, chaperone.

She'll also be our stylist since the internationally known fashion designer Blaine Blackwell is currently on a major project in Milan, Italy.

I texted everyone today to let them know we needed to have an important meeting by phone at

3:00 p.m. to discuss a potential project for our band. I didn't give them any details.

Everyone was LOVING their Savage Summer Challenges and staying SUPERbusy. So when I asked them about taking time off to participate in a band project, we got into a heated discussion.

"I think we should pass," Zoey said. "After that SUPERintense Bad Boyz tour, I think WE need a break too." Brandon totally agreed with Zoey.

"Are we going to be paid in cupcakes again?" Marc complained. "Right now I need cold hard cash to fund my motocross." Theo agreed with Marc.

"Sorry! But I totally REFUSE to share the stage with another creepy CLOWN!" Chloe grumped. "That was too weird!" Violet agreed with Chloe.

"Okay, we'll consider ALL of that. But I also need to figure out if we're even available. So, what do your schedules look like for the next two weeks?"

113

"This is HOPELESS!" Chloe complained. "We're WAY too busy to even agree on a date!"

Ironically, everyone enthusiastically AGREED that we'd NEVER agree.

"I totally understand how everyone feels," I said. "To address your concerns: Unfortunately, there's no pay. But there are no clowns or cupcakes either. It's a trip to a major city, mostly to CHILLAX, not work."

I continued. "I know you're all looking forward to your Savage Summer Challenge projects. But what if we were offered a once-in-a-lifetime luxury vacation? For FREE! Personally, I think we'd be STUPID not to take advantage of this opportunity!"

Ironically, everyone AGREED with THAT, too! Suddenly my friends all started talking at once.

And soon they were BEGGING me to tell them WHERE we were going and WHEN we'd be leaving.

"So, here are the deets!" I smiled. "Who's up for . . ."

My friends could NOT believe this FANTASTIC news!

"Listen up, guys. I'm SERIOUS! We leave for PARIS in exactly THREE days! Trevor has already cleared everything with our parents. So we should probably hang up and start packing. Right now!" I giggled.

Everything must have FINALLY started to sink into their brains, because suddenly my friends totally lost it and started yelling hysterically into their phones.

Chloe and Zoey both had the same reaction. . . .

"SQUEEEEEEEEEE!!" ☺!

"WOW! You have NO IDEA!! I've always DREAMED of going to PARIS!!" Violet gushed.

"Nikki, this is great news! PARIS is such a WONDERFUL city!" Brandon exclaimed. "And it's going to be even better being there with YOU! And, um . . . ALL our friends, of course!"

"Paris ROCKS! Practically everyone rides scooters there! How cool is that?!" Marc said.

"WHOA! Paris sounds GREAT! I love French cuisine, especially the pastries!" Theo practically drooled.

OMG! It was such a relief to FINALLY share this news with everyone. I've been keeping it a secret, like, forever, and it was KILLING me!

I explained all the details about our trip, and how other than our one-day photo shoot, we'd be able to spend most of our time exploring the city, visiting famous landmarks, and experiencing French culture.

This trip to Paris is going to be just . . .

AWESOME!!

I mean, WHAT could go WRONG?!!

FRIDAY, AUGUST 15

Yesterday I very naively and stupidly asked,
"WHAT COULD GO WRONG?!!"

Well, by 9:00 a.m. I had my answer!!

OMG! WHY does it seem like my life is just one
HUGE DISASTER waiting to happen ☹?!!

AAAAAAAHHHHH!!

That was me SCREAMING!!

I just got a text a few minutes ago with some
AWFUL news! Remember when I said we had the
same management team as before?

Unfortunately, we ALSO have the same shady,
manipulative, lazy, backstabbing, hopelessly vain,
conniving, fake-'n'-fabulous, lip-gloss-addicted
SOCIAL MEDIA INTERN! . . .

MACKENZIE

HOLLISTER ☹!

I couldn't believe it!

Our chaperone (and total ice queen), Victoria Steel, was actually giving that girl a second chance to cover our PARIS trip after the AWFUL job she did on the Bad Boyz tour!

Like, WHO does THAT?!!

Apparently, Victoria will be hiring a SECOND intern to help MacKenzie and also serve as our guide and interpreter while we're in Paris. Thank goodness!

I just hope this new person is actually competent and will do more than hang out at the spa, get manis and pedis, drink caramel macchiatos, eat at fancy restaurants, and shop.

UNLIKE MacKenzie!

But there was MORE bad news! Victoria explained that MacKenzie was SUPERexcited and wanted to meet with me today to discuss her social media plans for Paris.

MacKenzie's newest CCP (Cute, Cool & Popular) hangout is a trendy coffee shop located inside our local bookstore.

Victoria said MacKenzie wanted to meet me there today at noon.

JUST GREAT ☹!

I was VERY sure the LAST thing MacKenzie wanted to talk to me about today was her social media plans.

I tried my hardest to make up an excuse so I wouldn't have to waste my afternoon hanging out with that self-absorbed drama queen. But Victoria was our creative director, and she INSISTED!

My mom agreed to drop me off at the bookstore while she and Brianna visited the CupCakery for sweet treats.

I arrived at the bookstore ten minutes early and decided to check out the new books in the art and drawing section.

Luckily, I still had money from my birthday.

I just happened to stumble across the COOLEST book EVER, called Parisian Fashion Illustration. . . .

ME, FINDING A VERY COOL
FASHION ILLUSTRATION BOOK!

Back when I suggested our Savage Summer Challenge projects, my goal was to learn fashion illustration.

It's a beautiful and elegant style of drawing used to illustrate fashions like the fabulous designs you see on the runways in Paris, Milan, and NYC.

You know, the 100% authentic stuff that's REAL! NOT like my KNOCKOFF designer handbag.

Unfortunately, I never had time to pursue it. I was way too busy worrying about Paris and making sure everyone was available to make the trip!

Maybe this was something I could do after all! In PARIS! The fashion capital of the world!

I imagined myself sitting on a bench, sketching Parisians strolling through the park, while my crush, Brandon, took photos of the gorgeous cityscape.

Like, how ROMANTIC would THAT be?!

SQUEEEEEEEEEEEE ☺!!

ME, DREAMING OF CREATING
BEAUTIFUL FASHION ILLUSTRATIONS
WHILE I'M IN PARIS!

Suddenly my wonderful dream was rudely interrupted!

"Nikki? Hi, hon!" MacKenzie said as she sashayed down the aisle toward me like it was a Fashion Week runway. I just HATE it when that girl sashays!

Then she stopped dead in her tracks and stared at me.

"OMG! You're reading *Parisian Fashion Illustration?!*" she uttered in shock.

"Um . . . YEAH! I plan to buy it." I answered like it wasn't a big deal.

"But it's about cutting-edge fashion!" MacKenzie protested.

"I know that!" I said, rolling my eyes.

"But, Nikki, it doesn't have SILLY doodles, GOOFY cartoon characters, STUPID knock-knock jokes, or any of that other immature kiddie GARBAGE

126

you LOVE so much!" MacKenzie said as she took out her Scornfully Scathing Scarlet lip gloss and slathered on three layers. "Sorry, but you wouldn't understand a WORD you were reading, hon. Although you MIGHT enjoy looking at all the PRETTY pictures!"

I could NOT believe MacKenzie said all that right to my face like that. I stared into her cold, icy blue eyes.

"Speaking of GARBAGE, you're spewing a lot of TRASH TALK today, MacKenzie! Your nasty little problem is going to require an ammonia-flavored BREATH MINT sprinkled with those little Scrubbing Bubbles thingies! But you're gonna need the toilet bowl cleaner strength!"

MacKenzie looked at me like I was something her spoiled poodle, Fifi, had left in the grass in her backyard.

OMG! That girl is such a DRAMA QUEEN! She picked up a book and casually flipped through the pages. Then she smiled at me all evil-like and said . . .

MACKENZIE'S
NEW $900
DESIGNER
SHOES

"MacKenzie, please just get to the point!"
I sighed. "I already know this meeting has nothing
WHATSOEVER to do with your social media job."

"Actually, you're RIGHT! WHY would I waste my
time doing anything for YOU and your group of
no-talent misfits pretending to be a band?!"
MacKenzie sneered. "I'm going to have a GLAM
vacation in PARIS, and that WITCH, Victoria Steel,
is going to PAY ME while I'm doing it!"

"MacKenzie, that is SO dishonest! WHAT do you have
to say for yourself?!" I asked, totally disgusted.

"YAY, ME!" MacKenzie smirked.

I could NOT believe she actually said that.

"So, WHAT does your GLAM VACAY in Paris have to
do with ME?" I asked, already dreading her answer.

"I'm so happy you asked, Nikki! The Bad Boyz
haven't selected a new band member yet since
they're taking a break. That means there's STILL

a chance that spot could be MINE! But I'm going to need a much higher profile. I think appearing on the COVER of a FRENCH magazine could be just the thing I need to set me apart from all the wannabes! Trevor and the Bad Boyz need to see how talented and INCREDIBLY PHOTOGENIC I am!" she bragged.

I didn't know whether MacKenzie was shamelessly VAIN or just hopelessly DELUSIONAL!

"Sorry to disappoint you, MacKenzie! But my band and I are going to be featured on the cover of that magazine. I could be wrong, but I don't think your social media intern job description includes COVER MODEL. Anyway, I need to get home because I still have A LOT of packing to do. Good-bye!"

I turned around and headed toward the checkout to buy my fashion book and leave.

"NIKKI MAXWELL! COME BACK HERE! THIS MEETING ISN'T OVER UNTIL I SAY IT'S OVER!"
MacKenzie yelled at me.

That's when I noticed practically everyone in the bookstore was staring at us. MacKenzie smiled and sashayed over to me. I just HATE it when that girl sashays!

"Listen, Nikki, I need YOUR help to get that spot in the Bad Boyz, and YOU need MY help to get that trip to PARIS. So let's just agree to help each other," she said sweetly.

"I don't NEED anything from you!" I shot back.

"Really?! Well, I think you NEED me to NOT send this VIDEO to Trevor Chase! Once he sees it, there's NO WAY he's going to let you go to Paris to appear on the cover of a magazine. Your little friends will be DEVASTATED, and it'll be ALL YOUR fault! They're going to HATE YOU for the rest of your MISERABLE little life!"

"MacKenzie, Trevor said we earned that invitation to Paris! You're obviously just jealous. HOW could you do something so . . . CRUEL?!"

"EASY! Just WATCH me!" she snarled. . . .

MACKENZIE, ABOUT TO SEND THAT AWFUL VIDEO TO TREVOR!!

If I was the only person involved, I would've dealt with the consequences of that video.

I didn't deserve to go to Paris or be on any stage ever again! But my FRIENDS were involved, and they hadn't done anything wrong.

There was no way I was going to stand by and let MacKenzie DESTROY their DREAMS of visiting Paris!

Especially after they already canceled their Savage Summer Challenge activities.

They didn't DESERVE this!

So . . .

YES!!

I told MacKenzie that I would "think about" her taking my place on the cover just to keep her from sending that video to Trevor.

She told me I had to let her know my final decision the day before the cover shoot.

OR ELSE . . . !!

And I think that's a threat!!

I'm so UPSET and DISGUSTED right now,
I can barely write!

I've decided to keep all this a secret from my BFFs
until I figure a way out of this mess.

SORRY!

But I REFUSE to let this DRAMA QUEEN
RUIN our trip to PARIS!

☹!

SATURDAY, AUGUST 16

I can't believe Chloe and Zoey are already packed!!
I haven't even STARTED yet!

My only hope is that there is something PERFECT
for my trip to Paris in the Mount Everest of dirty
clothes piled on my bed. . . .

ME, JUST CHILLAXING DURING A SERIOUS
PERSONAL LAUNDRY CRISIS!

Yes, I KNOW! I'm supposed to leave for Paris in twenty-four hours!

But I STILL need to do several GIGANTIC loads of laundry before I can even THINK about packing.

OMG! I'm so DISGUSTED with my MOM! She has been NO help WHATSOEVER!!

She said if I am OLD enough to cross the Atlantic Ocean without her, I'm OLD enough to pour laundry detergent into a washing machine!

So I was SUPERhappy when Chloe and Zoey volunteered to come over and help me do my laundry and pack.

They're the BEST friends EVER ☺!

I ran down to the kitchen to grab some snacks while they got started.

And when I returned with chips, dip, and sodas, they were both frantically digging through my closet. . . .

CHLOE AND ZOEY, FRANTICALLY
SEARCHING FOR MY COSTUME!

Obviously, my BFFs had just overlooked it or something. I specifically REMEMBER keeping my costume hidden from Brianna in the back of my closet. Until that day I . . .

OMG! WHAT HAVE I DONE?!!

I was so UPSET and ANGRY at myself, I wanted
to just . . .

SCREAM!!

WHAT. WAS. I. THINKING?! I didn't have
a choice but to tell my BFFs the awful TRUTH!

"CHLOE AND ZOEY, I HAVE TERRIBLE NEWS!"
I groaned. "YOU'RE NOT GONNA BELIEVE THIS!"

They both plopped on top of my bed and eagerly
helped themselves to the snacks.

"Um . . . let me guess!" Zoey said as she took a sip
of soda. "You lost your luggage, and it's somewhere
buried in this pile of dirty clothes?!"

I just rolled my eyes. Very funny!

"NO?" Chloe giggled as she stuffed her face with
chips. "Your dog, DAISY, disappeared three days ago,
and you think SHE might be lost somewhere in this
pile of clothes?!"

"This is no time for JOKES!" I complained. "I'm very SERIOUS!!"

"Okay, sorry!" Zoey said, trying to keep a straight face. "It's BRIANNA who's missing and lost in this HUGE pile of dirty clothes!! Have you filed a missing person report yet?!"

My BFFs laughed and gave each other a high five. That's when I practically yelled at them, "You're NOT going to believe this, but my stage costume isn't in the closet! It's, um . . . MISSING! Guys, I'm in really BIG TROUBLE!"

Chloe and Zoey just stared at me with their mouths dangling open.

"YOUR COSTUME IS MISSING AND BURIED SOMEWHERE IN THIS HUGE PILE OF DIRTY CLOTHES?!" Chloe asked, totally confused. "ARE YOU SERIOUS?!"

"Well, can't we just dig it out?!" Zoey reasoned. "It's GOTTA be in there somewhere!"

"_NO!_ You don't understand. Brianna made a joke about me almost falling offstage, and I got really mad. So I . . . I, um . . . TOSSED my costume!"

"INTO THE PILE OF DIRTY CLOTHES?!" Chloe and Zoey asked in unison.

"_NOOO!_" I shrieked. I took a deep breath and tried to compose myself. "I'm really embarrassed to admit this. But I kind of threw it away in the, um . . . GARBAGE BIN in the garage!"

"GARBAGE BIN?!" they gasped.

"_Okay, wait a minute! You had a HISSY FIT and MELTDOWN about a little joke . . . ?!_" Chloe began.

"_. . . And threw a one-of-a-kind, expensive, designer stage costume in the TRASH?!_" Zoey finished.

"Unfortunately, I . . . DID! I guess I was having a really BAD day! Guys, I'm SO SORRY!"

Suddenly my eyes filled up with tears. That's when

Chloe and Zoey grabbed me and we did a group hug together.

"Well, Nikki, if you threw it away, we'll just go down to the garage and get it!" Zoey reassured me.

"Problem solved!" Chloe said, flashing jazz hands.

I couldn't believe my BFFs were being SO supportive. They weren't even mad at me! We were about to rush downstairs to the garage when Chloe stopped and stared out my window. "Um, Nikki, your garbage pickup is today, right?" she asked, scrunching up her face.

I had TOTALLY forgotten about that!

"Actually, it is!" I answered. "We'd better get down to that garbage bin before it's too late!"

"I have some really bad news!" Chloe muttered. "I think it might ALREADY be too late . . . !"

Zoey and I ran to the window and peeked out. Then we gasped and stared in disbelief! . . .

MY BFFS AND ME, WATCHING IN HORROR
AS A TRUCK DUMPS MY GARBAGE!

We pounded on my window and screamed at the tops of our lungs to try to get the driver's attention. . . .

"STOP! STOOOP!! STOOOOP!!!"

But the truck was making so much noise ROARING, GRINDING, CLANKING, and THUMPING that he didn't hear us.

"COME ON! WE HAVE TO TRY TO STOP HIM BEFORE IT'S TOO LATE! RUN!!" Zoey shouted as she bolted for the door and bounded down the stairs.

Chloe and I followed close behind her.

Our street must have been the last stop or something because by the time we got outside, that garbage truck had completely DISAPPEARED!

I stumbled out to the bin in shock, muttering to myself, "My costume! My costume! I need my costume for PARIS!!"

I'll admit, I totally LOST IT! AGAIN!! . . .

ME, LOOKING FOR MY COSTUME!!

I couldn't believe that HIDEOUS MONSTER of a truck had actually EATEN my stage costume!

Right before my EYES! I was TRAUMATIZED!!

For a moment I thought I had gotten dizzy and blacked out from the ANGUISH of the HORRIFIC thing I had just witnessed.

But then I realized I was UPSIDE DOWN in the BOTTOM of that pitch-dark garbage bin, literally SCREAMING MY HEAD OFF! . . .

"NOOOOOOOOO!!"

OMG! You have no idea how DARK and SCARY it was inside there.

And then I started gagging because I could barely BREATHE!! It was very stinky, too!

Like two-week-old rotten eggs.

Only ten times WORSE!

I was so HAPPY Chloe and Zoey grabbed me by my ankles and pulled me out of that garbage bin.

I wanted to give them a big hug for saving my life! But they told me not to touch them because I smelled like rotten eggs. Only ten times WORSE!

I think they were also a little grossed out because I had green slime in my hair, and it was dripping down the side of my face. EWW!

But Chloe and Zoey said not to worry because they were going to take care of everything.

They explained that my job was to chillax, take a long, hot shower to get rid of that awful garbage smell, and start packing for our trip to Paris.

I am SO lucky to have Chloe and Zoey in my life. Now they just need to find that garbage truck and get my costume back!

Like, how hard can that be?! ☺!!

SUNDAY, AUGUST 17

TODAY IS THE MOST EXCITING DAY OF MY
ENTIRE LIFE!

I can't believe I'll be leaving for the airport at
noon. SQUEEEEEEEE ☺!!

I was so traumatized by that garbage truck fiasco
yesterday that I took a hot shower and slept most
of the day.

So I got up SUPERearly this morning and washed,
like, nine loads of laundry.

Actually, it was only TWO loads of laundry. But
STILL!! It felt like nine.

It's only 8:30 a.m., and I'm totally exhausted!

To save time and energy, I just started grabbing
clothes and literally tossing them into my suitcase.

So now I'm almost done packing. . . .

ME, PACKING MY
SUITCASE FOR PARIS!

I finally got a text from Chloe and Zoey with an update about my costume. The sanitation company had good news and bad news.

The good news is that they know where my dress is located ☺! It's buried somewhere in a twenty-acre landfill.

However, the bad news is that they weren't able to find and return my dress to me because it's buried somewhere in a twenty-acre landfill ☹!

My BFFs told me not to worry because they were going to come up with a plan once we got to Paris. But how can I NOT worry about something as important as the DRESS I'm supposed to wear?!

Anyway, I'd FINALLY finished packing and placed my luggage in the hall so my dad could take it downstairs, when Brianna peeped into my room. I was expecting her to ask me something very selfish, like if she could have my room. Hey, I was going to Paris for twelve days, NOT to college for four years. But Brianna totally surprised me. . . .

ME, TRYING MY BEST NOT TO CRY!

Brianna handed me her fave Princess Sugar Plum backpack. She said it had a gift inside just for me!

BRIANNA GAVE ME THE WORST GOING-AWAY
PRESENT IN THE HISTORY OF MANKIND!

"But, Nikki, you don't understand!" Brianna protested. "My teddy bear, Hans, is from PARIS! He speaks French and wants to visit his family!"

"Brianna, Hans is NOT from PARIS! Dad got him at a neighbor's garage sale along with a busted toaster for only $2.00. It took Mom an entire week to finally get rid of that AWFUL smell."

"Hey, it's not MY fault Dad's TOASTER smelled like dirty gym socks!!" Brianna shot back.

"The toaster didn't smell. HANS did! He reeked!! Even worse than the boys' locker room at school!" I explained. "No way am I dragging Hans around PARIS in a pink Princess Sugar Plum backpack!"

I gave Brianna her bear and backpack, quickly shoved all THREE of them out of my room, slammed my door shut, and locked it.

BANG! BANG! BANG!

JUST GREAT! Now Brianna was pounding on my door.

"But, Nikki, there's MORE! It's a MAGICAL surprise! You're gonna LOVE IT!! I promise!"

"Thanks, Brianna, but right now I have a plane to catch. How about I see it when I get back from Paris, okay?!" I yelled through the door.

"NO! YOU NEED TO TAKE HANS AND MY BACKPACK TO PARIS WITH YOU!! OR YOU'RE GOING TO BE SORRY!!" she shouted.

Then Brianna was mysteriously quiet. I thought she'd left my door until I heard my dad in the hallway.

"Brianna, can you help me take Nikki's luggage downstairs? You grab the carry-on, and I'll take this big one, okay, honey?"

I glanced at the clock. The driver was picking me up in less than an hour, and I STILL needed to change my clothes. I decided to wear my FAVE summer dress with cute sandals on the plane. When I finally came downstairs, my entire family was there waiting for me! . . .

ME, SAYING GOOD-BYE TO MY FAMILY!

I have to admit, I got a huge lump in my throat and felt like I was going to cry when everyone was hugging me good-bye.

It was hard to believe this was actually happening. I was FINALLY on my way to PARIS with my best friends. It was a DREAM come true!

Not even MacKenzie could ruin this wonderful moment.

I was waiting at the front door with my luggage when the car pulled into my driveway. My friends lowered the tinted windows, smiled, and waved at me excitedly.

I was about to embark on the adventure of a lifetime!

In PARIS! And I was MORE than ready!

SQUEEEEEEEEEE!!

☺!!

WARNING!

This is going to be one of my LONGEST diary entries EVER!!

But that's because of the RIDICULOUS amount of DRAMA I've had to deal with in the past twenty-four hours!

So hang on! It's going to be a roller-coaster ride!

Trevor had arranged for my bandmates and me to fly FIRST CLASS along with Victoria Steel.

I COULDN'T WAIT to sit in those large comfy seats while the flight attendants spoiled us with warm, freshly baked cookies and a cold glass of milk. YUM!!

But the most exciting thing about our trip was that Brandon and I had seats next to each other!

SQUEEEE 😊!!

The nonstop flight to Paris was going to be seven hours and fifteen minutes, which meant Brandon and I could talk FOREVER!

Thank goodness MacKenzie was seated in coach. I didn't have to worry about her sticking her bronzed and contoured little NOSE in MY business!

I was the last person in line to get my boarding pass and check my bags when I suddenly realized my passport wasn't in my purse!

YIKES ☹!

HOW could I have MISPLACED my passport?! I thought maybe I had stuck it in a jacket pocket, but it wasn't there, either. I was so upset, I was about to burst into tears!

Since our plane to Paris was boarding in less than an hour, Chloe and Zoey stayed behind to help me look for it while Victoria and everyone else headed for security screening and our gate.

"Don't worry, Nikki!" Chloe said. "We'll find your passport!"

"Let's check inside your luggage. I'm sure it's in there somewhere!" Zoey assured me.

OMG!! I was ALWAYS losing things!

You know, like my diary, party invites, an expensive stage costume, and NOW my passport.

We found a spot on the floor and zipped open my luggage.

There was GOOD news and BAD news.

The GOOD NEWS was that we found my passport! In my mad rush to pack, I'd stuck it in my luggage.

The BAD NEWS was that I accidentally discovered a mysterious DISASTER of EPIC proportions!! . . .

That's when I closed my eyes and screamed . . .

"BRIANNA, HOW COULD YOU DO THIS TO ME?!!"

But I just said that inside my head, so no one else heard it but me!

Hey, those scary-looking TSA officers were watching us.

The last thing I wanted was to get arrested for "disturbing the peace" or "having an extreme hissy fit in public" and MISS my flight to Paris!

The ONLY items in my suitcase were my pajamas, bunny slippers, toothbrush, and socks, along with Brianna's backpack and FAKE-French teddy bear!

I was so DISGUSTED! I was going to be in Paris, the FASHION capital of the world, for twelve days! But thanks to Brianna, the ONLY outfit I had made me look like an adorably cute, sloppy-chic, sleep-deprived . . . CLOWN!! . . .

ME, HANGING OUT WITH HANS,
WEARING MY PJ'S, BUNNY SLIPPERS,
AND THREE PAIRS OF SOCKS ☹!

I called my parents and left a FRANTIC message. . . .

"Hi, this is Nikki, and it's an EMERGENCY! All the clothes I packed are MISSING from my luggage! I think Brianna might have taken them. Could you please find my clothes and bring them to me here at the airport ASAP?! I'll be waiting at Door Seven. Thanks! Love you!"

I was praying they got my message!

But I'd overheard Brianna begging my parents to take her to see the new movie *Princess Sugar Plum Saves Baby Unicorn Island, Part 11.*

So it was very possible my family was at the movie theater and my call went straight to voice mail.

Chloe, Zoey, and I were anxiously waiting at Door 7 for my parents to arrive with a life-saving emergency clothing delivery, when we heard a shocking announcement over the PA system that shook us to our core. . . .

"FLIGHT 9257 TO PARIS, FRANCE, IS NOW BOARDING AT GATE EIGHTEEN. BUSINESS AND FIRST-CLASS PASSENGERS ARE INVITED TO BEGIN BOARDING AT THIS TIME. THANK YOU."

The three of us froze and gasped!

"OMG! Our plane is BOARDING!!" I shrieked. "Chloe and Zoey, you'd better get going!"

"Are you KA-RAY-ZEE?!" Chloe blurted out. "We're not going ANYWHERE! What about your clothes?!"

"Nikki, we're not leaving unless YOU come with US!" Zoey exclaimed. "We're staying TOGETHER!!"

My BFFs tried to argue with me, but I was NOT having it. My clothing emergency had to wait.

"SORRY! But NO WAY are you guys missing this flight to PARIS! I still need to check my luggage. So I'll just meet you both at the gate. Now, PLEASE GO! And HURRY!!" I shouted.

Finally convinced, my BFFs gave me a reassuring hug and took off running.

I slid the backpack over my shoulder, grabbed my luggage, and hurried back to the baggage check counter. Luckily, there wasn't a line at first class.

The attendant stared at her watch. "Both you and your luggage are late," she said. "So you'll need to hurry if you want to catch that plane. Good luck!"

My next stop was security screening. But FIRST I desperately needed to DITCH Hans and the Princess Sugar Plum backpack. I REFUSED to drag that DUMB bear all the way to PARIS!! Brianna would just have to get over it!

I rushed into the nearest restroom and waited impatiently until it was mostly empty. Then, as soon as an elderly woman closed her stall door, I stealthily completed my SECRET MISSION! . . .

I STUFFED HANS AND THE
PRINCESS SUGAR PLUM BACKPACK
INTO A TRASH CAN AND TOOK OFF RUNNING
TO TRY TO CATCH MY PLANE!!

Since we were flying to Paris on a humongous 747 jumbo jet, boarding could take quite a while.

Chloe and Zoey had probably made it to the gate by now and were already aboard the plane.

I was very confident I'd be joining my BFFs soon! UNTIL I heard another disturbing announcement:

"THIS IS THE FINAL BOARDING CALL FOR PASSENGER NICOLE J. MAXWELL FOR FLIGHT 9257 TO PARIS, FRANCE. PLEASE PROCEED TO GATE EIGHTEEN IMMEDIATELY. THE DOORS OF THE AIRCRAFT WILL CLOSE IN APPROXIMATELY TEN MINUTES! AGAIN, THIS IS THE FINAL BOARDING CALL FOR NICOLE J. MAXWELL. THANK YOU!"

OMG! I was going to miss that plane! I had only ten minutes . . . no, actually nine minutes . . . to get through security and to Gate 18!

I didn't think my HORRIBLE situation could get ANY worse. But somehow it always does! . . .

ME, SHOCKED AND
SURPRISED TO SEE MY BEAR
AND BACKPACK AGAIN ☹!!

I mustered a smile and said, "It was very kind of you to return them to me. Thank you SO much!"

But as soon as she walked away, I scanned the area for a trash bin to toss my stuff. AGAIN!

I spotted one close by, but a burly TSA officer was standing near it. He didn't appear to be the sensitive type who could relate to a teen girl desperate to dispose of worthless junk her bratty little sister had secretly stashed in her luggage. So I quickly decided it would be prudent to hang on to everything, at least until I arrived in Paris.

After I finally got through security, I ran all the way to Gate 18! All passengers had boarded, and a woman was about to close the door to the jetway.

When I told her my name, she took my boarding pass and escorted me to the plane. I could hardly believe I'd actually made it! SQUEEEEE ☺!!!

OMG! I was SO happy to see everyone again! But Victoria was obviously NOT very happy to see ME! . . .

My bandmates were just as confused as I was.

They stared in shock and disbelief.

"MacKenzie, you actually think I should be FIRED and SENT HOME just because I'm a little late?! I got here before the plane left!" I exclaimed.

"NO! You should be FIRED and SENT HOME because that teddy bear of yours is so CREEPY that forcing us to look at it is CRUEL AND UNUSUAL PUNISHMENT!!" MacKenzie sneered. "Nikki, how do you even sleep at night with that thing?! It has the face of a Chucky doll and the body of a rotting muskrat!!"

"For your information, it's not MY bear!! It's BRIANNA'S!" I shot back.

"OMG! You STOLE your little sister's teddy bear?! Girlfriend, you need SERIOUS help!"

"I DIDN'T steal it! I FOUND it! But it's a complicated story, MacKenzie. If I had more time, I'd explain

172

it with sock puppets and nursery rhymes so you'd understand!" I muttered.

"Listen, you don't have to LIE about your obsession with your teddy bear and Princess Sugar Plum backpack! I mean, you're carrying them around in broad daylight. To be honest, I think it would be adorable. IF you were still FOUR years old!" MacKenzie smirked.

"WOULD ALL PASSENGERS PLEASE TAKE YOUR SEATS, FASTEN YOUR SEAT BELTS, AND PREPARE FOR TAKEOFF!" a flight attendant announced over the PA system.

"I guess that means YOU!" MacKenzie said rudely as she waved good-bye. "By the way, MY seat is . . . Oops! I meant to say . . . YOUR seat is 25D. Have fun in coach, hon! TOODLES!"

MacKenzie had just TOODLED me?! I was SO angry, I could just . . . SPIT!! And she was in MY seat! But that wasn't even the WORST part! She was SITTING next to MY crush, BRANDON!! While I was SITTING next to . . .

173

. . . A TASMANIAN DEVIL DISGUISED AS A THREE-YEAR-OLD SPOILED BRAT!!

OMG! That kid made Brianna look like Miss Manners!

My seat was so STICKY and GERMY from his assortment of snacks, juices, and toys, I wanted to ask the flight attendant for a moist towelette, a can of LYSOL, and a HAZMAT SUIT! And we hadn't even left the runway yet!

"AAAAAHHHHH!!"

That was me SCREAMING in frustration! But I just did it inside my head, so no one else heard it but me!

I'll be very lucky if I even SURVIVE this trip to PARIS!! So far it was a TOTAL DISASTER!

In just an hour I'd LOST:

1. my first-class seat

2. my clothing I'd packed for this trip

3. my self-esteem

4. the respect of my creative director, Victoria

5. my patience with MacKenzie.

Just then I got a text, and it was from . . .

BRANDON

I'm really sorry
we didn't get to
sit together. But
we're going to
have the BEST
time ever in Paris.
I promise! TMB

OMG! I was NOT expecting that! I had a million
butterflies fluttering around in my stomach!

My cheeks felt flushed, and my palms were sticky.

And it had nothing whatsoever to do with the fact that that bratty little kid had just dumped his entire sippy cup of juice over my HEAD.

I was finally on my way to PARIS!

It felt like I had been DREAMING about this day FOREVER!!

And Brandon actually wrote "TMB," which means . . .

"Text me back!"

SQUEEEEEEEEEE!
☺!!

I'll admit I was in a horrible mood when I got on that plane. But yesterday I arrived at the Charles de Gaulle Airport with a brand-new attitude!

BONJOUR, PARIS ☺!

The one perk of sitting near a crying TODDLER for the entire flight was that I could NOT sleep! So I spent seven hours brushing up on my French. . . .

Je m'appelle Nikki! That means "My name is Nikki!"

J'adore Paris! That means "I love Paris!"

See how GOOD I am?!

"We made it!" Chloe and Zoey squealed as we stepped out of the airport and into the French air.

Maybe it was just my imagination, but I could actually smell freshly baked croissants, designer perfume fragrances, and, um . . . artists' oil paint.

Inspired by renowned French artists like Monet, Degas, Rodin, Lenoir, and Delacroix, I decided to take my OWN art to the next level by trying the new fashion illustration style. I'll sign my new artwork

Nicole J. Maxwell

which looks VERY chic, artsy, and . . . FRENCH ☺!

We piled into two shiny black vans and headed for our hotel. According to the brochure in the folder Victoria had given us, it was within walking distance of the Eiffel Tower. YES! THE EIFFEL TOWER!!

Once we arrived at L'Hôtel Magnifique de Paris, we gasped and just stared at the place in total awe. Calling it magnificent was an understatement! I pinched myself to make sure I wasn't dreaming.

We rushed out of the van, and Brandon grabbed his camera and started snapping photos.

After several buses filled with tourists left the hotel, he took a photo of Chloe, Zoey, and me in front of a gorgeous fountain at the main entrance. . . .

Nicole J. Maxwell

We did a group hug and smiled for the camera. . . .

OMG!! Our dream of visiting Paris together had FINALLY come true!

"Okay, nobody move a muscle!" MacKenzie shouted as she rushed toward us. "Please, stay right there!"

We stared at her, pleasantly surprised. Although she was our social media intern, she rarely took any photos, except to humiliate us. Was PARIS already having a positive impact on MacKenzie?!

"I need to keep this sidewalk clear. For my LUGGAGE! So stay out of the way!" she sneered.

NOPE! Paris was turning her into an even BIGGER drama queen. Trailing behind her were two bellhops from the hotel struggling to push a cart piled high with a teetering stack of designer luggage.

OMG! I could NOT even imagine the STRESS of traveling with NINE pieces of luggage stuffed with expensive clothing, shoes, and jewelry! But I was mature and savvy enough to deal with that situation IF it became absolutely necessary. . . .

ME, FORCED TO TRAVEL WITH PILES
OF DESIGNER LUGGAGE STUFFED WITH
EXPENSIVE CLOTHING, SHOES, AND JEWELRY!

What can I say?! I'm a VERY disciplined person.

As MacKenzie brushed past us, Zoey couldn't hide her frustration. "Um . . . MacKenzie! Where are you going? You're supposed to be documenting this trip for our social media campaign," she complained.

Trevor Chase had specifically instructed her to take lots of photos. He thought behind—the—scenes shots and footage would help us build our brand on social media and increase our number of followers.

"YEAH, RIGHT!" MacKenzie scoffed. "I'd rather document MOLD growing on lunch meat than spend my vacation time taking pictures of YOU three losers. *Excusez—moi.* As soon as I drop off my luggage, I'm going SHOPPING! So . . . toodles!"

I could not believe MacKenzie actually TOODLED us right to our FACES like that!

Does she NOT realize that WE are the reason she is here in PARIS giving those poor bellhops HERNIAS by forcing them to push her 639 pounds of designer LUGGAGE?!

Some people are SO ungrateful!!

The lavish hotel lobby looks like the inside of a palace. It has plush red carpet with gorgeous antique gold furniture that glistens under the light from three huge chandeliers, each with over a hundred bulbs!

I held my breath as Victoria took out her iPad to announce our room assignments.

I guess I was STILL pretty traumatized from having to share a room with a lip-gloss-addicted WEASEL on our last tour ☹!

Thank goodness I got assigned to a suite with Chloe and Zoey this time around. And Violet was lucky to get a single bedroom in the suite she's sharing with Victoria and MacKenzie.

Victoria and MacKenzie are actually roommates. Hey, those two TOTALLY deserve each other.

Under Victoria's watchful eye, MacKenzie is actually going to have to WORK as an intern instead of just shopping, eating at trendy restaurants, and hanging out at the spa all day long!

Chloe, Zoey, and I are sharing a gorgeous two-bedroom suite.

And my wonderful BFFs INSISTED that I take the single room while they share the double.

"Nikki, you totally deserve that room!" Zoey insisted.

"You're the reason we're ALL here!" Chloe gushed.

Hey, I couldn't argue with THAT!

Anyway, my hotel room is ~~SO MAGNIFICENT~~ *TRÈS MAGNIFIQUE!*

And that brochure was correct. I can actually see the Eiffel Tower from my room!!

SQUEEEEEE ☺!!! . . .

I LOVE PARIS!

Nicole J. Maxwell

After exploring my hotel suite and taking a ton of photos, I finally called my family to let them know I had safely arrived in Paris.

They said they were already missing me even though I'd barely been gone for twenty-four hours. Then my mom gave me some shocking news!

"Nikki, I'm SO sorry Brianna took most of your clothing out of your luggage to make room for her teddy bear! She said something about him having a magical surprise for you. Anyway, sweetheart, remember that debit card I gave you in case of an emergency? Please use it to replace everything that's missing. Okay?"

Then she gave me the name of a popular store in Paris called Mon Amour that specializes in TRENDY teen clothing at a really good price. I could even shop online and pick up my order at a nearby store.

I had to admit, I DID feel a little, um . . . GUILTY.

So I tried my hardest to convince my mom she DIDN'T need to buy me a bunch of NEW clothes! . . .

Anyway, I cannot believe that my embarrassingly frugal mother—who darns the holes in my old socks to give away as hand-me-downs to my thankless cousins—is actually FORCING me to SHOP.

How **KA-RAY-ZEE** is that?!!

It's like, *POOF!* I'm getting a chic new wardrobe in PARIS, the fashion capital of the world!

<u>OMG!</u> Brianna is a powerful MAGICIAN after all!

Since everyone was exhausted and jet-lagged, we spent the day relaxing, had dinner in our rooms, and turned in early.

The last thing I remember was lying in my comfy bed, staring out of my window, hypnotized by the EIFFEL TOWER glistening in the darkness! I sighed in awe, whispered, *"J'adore Paris,"* and blissfully dozed off to sleep.

☺!

I know this is going to sound a little weird, but I just realized my diary is as JET-LAGGED as I am!

So today I'm going to bring my entries up to date.

Everyone was so exhausted, we actually slept until NOON yesterday.

Then we spent the rest of the day in SUPERboring meetings with Victoria. Trevor joined us via Zoom.

He said we'll be doing a cover photo shoot and interview for the most popular teen magazine in France, *Oh Là Là Chic!*, on Thursday, August 28.

SQUEEEEEEEEEEEEEEEEE ☺!!

But get this!

Other than a few random meetings, my bandmates and I will only be working ONE DAY while we're in Paris!

Can you believe it?!

However, MacKenzie will be so busy, she's getting an assistant intern to help her with her workload. Sorry, NOT sorry!

Our parents signed a permission slip for us to tour the city as long as we clear all activities with our chaperone, Victoria, AND follow a long list of rules.

Trevor is covering all our expenses, and we each get a small stipend to spend each day.

Anyway, it's hard to believe it's already Wednesday and we've been in Paris TWO days!

We're SUPERexcited because we're FINALLY free to leave our hotel and start exploring the city.

SQUEEEEEEEEEE ☺!!

Everyone is DYING to do all the most Paris-y things that Paris has to offer.

Chloe, Zoey, and Violet decided to visit a café two blocks from our hotel, and I agreed to meet them there.

It's called

LE PETIT CAFÉ,

which means "The Little Coffee Shop."

The good news is that all the cramming I did on the plane is going to pay off because now I can speak FRENCH with the locals.

Like, how HARD can it be?!

By the time I arrived, Chloe, Zoey, and Violet had already ordered.

They were sitting outside at a fancy table, sipping their drinks, looking very POSH.

They offered to go inside with me, but I was VERY sure I could order my coffee myself. . . .

"Non, merci. Je reviens tout de suite." I smiled and
hurried inside.

Not to brag, but my French skillz are so good, I was impressing MYSELF!

I was expecting the French people there to be dressed from head to toe in the trendiest designer stuff right down to their LOUIS VUITTON loafers and CHANEL key chains.

So I was surprised everyone looked like they'd rolled out of bed and thrown on whatever wrinkled clothing they happened to find lying on the floor. I had no idea how they pulled this off.

Whenever I try to do shabby chic, it looks like I raided the lost and found box from my PE class. But when the French do it, it looks . . . um . . . *très chic!*

I waited in line and attempted to blend in by NOT smiling (also very FRENCH)!

Sorry, but if I lived in Paris, I would be smiling all the time!! WHY?! Because I'd be insanely happy I lived in Paris instead of Westchester, New York!!

DUH!!

Anyway, in my head I practiced how to order my favorite drink, an iced caramel cappuccino with whipped cream and extra caramel.

When it was finally my turn, I smiled, stepped up to the counter, and . . .

My mind went completely blank!

I could NOT believe this was happening to me!

"Je voudrais que vous sentiez mes pieds," I muttered nervously to the bored-looking French barista.

"Pardon?" She raised her eyebrows at me.

"Errr . . ." I hadn't expected any follow-up questions.

So I repeated myself, but much more slowly and loudly, like I was talking to my Grandma Maxwell. . . .

197

ME, TRYING TO ORDER AN ICED
CARAMEL CAPPUCCINO IN FRENCH

That's when the barista gasped and just stared at me. . . .

OMG! It was almost like she smelled something really bad. I resisted the urge to secretly sniff my armpits.

"*Oh là là là là là!!*" she huffed, glaring at me.

And I was all, "*UMMMM . . . . ?!!*" Was THIS how cafés worked in Paris?!

Suddenly Ms. French Barista grabbed a dishrag and started shooing me while yelling, "*T'ES GROSSIÈRE, MÉCHANTE!*"

I had no idea what she was screaming at me. But I totally understood the international gesture for . . . SCRAM!

So I slowly backed away from her.

I didn't think ordering coffee could possibly be more TRAUMATIC! Until a guy—I think he was the manager—came out of the kitchen and chased me out of the café with a BROOM! . . .

ME, LEAVING THE CAFÉ
IN A REALLY BIG RUSH!

Unfortunately, I DIDN'T get my iced caramel cappuccino with whipped cream and extra caramel ☹!

I hurried out of the café and returned to my friends empty-handed.

I could NOT believe they were all up in my business, asking me very personal questions like . . . "Where's your coffee?!" "Nikki, are you okay?!" "What happened in there?!"

"I think I messed up my order or something," I sighed. "And the barista must have been having a bad day because she totally freaked out. Then the manager came out and asked me to leave . . . kind of!"

"WHAT?!!" my friends exclaimed, totally confused.

"OMG! What exactly did you say to the barista?" Chloe asked.

"Je voudrais que vous sentiez mes pieds." I shrugged.

Violet cringed. "Nikki, please tell me you're joking!"

What I meant to say . . .

What I said . . .

OMG! I WAS SOOOO EMBARRASSED!!

I wanted to dig a really deep hole, crawl into it, and . . .

DIE ☹!!

"Seriously?! YOU actually told the barista to SMELL your FEET?!" Zoey giggled.

My friends laughed so hard, they had tears in their eyes.

ARRRRRRRRRRGH!!

Translation: I guess my French still needs a little work. Actually . . . A LOT of work!!

"Joking aside, just hang in there," Violet said sympathetically. "Before you know it, you'll be speaking like a Parisian!"

"Girlfriend, you got this!" Chloe agreed.

"I have an idea!" Zoey exclaimed. "Let's go back in there! We'll HELP you place your order!"

"Thanks, but no thanks," I muttered. "I've completely lost my appetite for a coffee."

"Okay, then just get a water," Chloe suggested. "It'll be a lot easier to order than an iced caramel cappuccino with whipped cream and extra caramel."

I had to admit that Chloe had a really good point.

"WATER?! That sounds nice," I agreed. "And now that I think about it, all this DRAMA has made me REALLY thirsty!"

I felt a surge of confidence as I realized I could easily get water. You know, like a REAL Parisian. Without any help WHATSOEVER from my friends.

They grabbed their drinks to go back inside the café, but I hurried off in the opposite direction. . . .

ME, GETTING WATER LIKE
A REAL PARISIAN!

I was SO thirsty, I practically guzzled THREE gallons of water.

I really appreciated my friends being supportive and offering to help me order in the café.

But . . . SORRY!!

I was NOT setting foot in that SCARY place again!!

There was no drink in the world I wanted badly enough to risk getting brutally SLAPPED with a dishrag and BEATEN DOWN with a broom!

Besides, the water fountain was FREE. And SAFE!

We sat outside at the café giggling and excitedly making a list of the places we each planned to visit while in Paris. Here is MY list:

1. Eiffel Tower

2. Louvre Museum

3. Arc de Triomphe

4. Sennelier art store

Anyway, today I learned an important lesson.
I REALLY need to work on my French.

Or someone is going to end up in very serious
trouble!

Namely . . .

MOI!!

☹!!

THURSDAY, AUGUST 21

On Tuesday I spent two hours shopping online for new clothing. It was a total BLAST!

I ordered the CUTEST outfits! But the best part is that everything was so reasonably priced.

Well, I JUST received an e-mail that my order is ready for pickup!! SQUEEEEEEEE ☺!!

Thank goodness Chloe, Zoey, and Violet were generous enough to loan me clothing this morning, or I'd STILL be wearing the same DRESS I arrived in.

I know . . . total YUCK ☹!

Because I'm a very mature and responsible young adult, I realized that picking up my clothing was a vital task that needed to be completed ASAP.

The store is about five miles away from my hotel. So I was googling directions to get there when I received a text message.

I was pleasantly surprised to see it was from BRANDON ☺! . . .

BRANDON

Hey, Nikki,
The restaurant here
has some of the best
ice cream in Paris. So
let's make plans to
hang out together and
talk ASAP. My treat!
Please say yes!

I had to make a difficult decision!

Do I hang out with my cute crush or go pick up the new clothing I'll need to wear for the next week?

Especially since the ONLY clean thing left in my suitcase is ONE sock.

The answer was obvious! I texted Brandon back. . . .

NIKKI

Thanks, Brandon! This sounds perfect! I'll meet you there in 30 minutes. See you soon!

SQUEEEEEEEEE ☺!!

What can I say?

I guess I'm NOT as mature and responsible as I thought I was. Since the swanky restaurant has a dress code, I didn't have a choice but to wear my dress. AGAIN!

I sprayed half a bottle of perfume on it just in case it was still a little smelly from my flight.

Then I brushed my hair, slathered on my FAVE lip gloss, and took the elevator down to the restaurant.

Brandon was already there waiting for me.

When he saw me, a huge smile spread across his face and he nervously brushed his shaggy bangs out of his eyes.

OMG! It kind of felt like we were on a date ☺!

Only we WEREN'T ☹!

I think just being in PARIS made EVERYTHING feel SUPERspecial.

The maître d' seated us at the perfect table for two.

It was on a dreamy balcony overlooking a beautiful flower garden full of butterflies flittering in the gentle breeze while birds tweeted in harmony.

212

OMG! It was so . . . ROMANTIC!

Until we were rudely interrupted by a very familiar voice SCREECHING at us from across the room!! . . .

"YOO-HOO! BRANDON AND NIKKI! DON'T YOU TWO DARE SIT THERE ALL ALONE! COME AND JOIN US! WE INSIST! S'IL VOUS PLAÎT!"

OMG!

It was MACKENZIE!!

She was seated at a table with Victoria, and it looked like they were having a meeting or something.

Brandon and I immediately panicked and stared at each other in sheer horror. We watched helplessly as MacKenzie scampered over to us like an . . . overexcited . . . mangy little . . . SQUIRREL . . . foaming at the mouth with . . . RABIES!

"OMG, Nikki! Are you STILL wearing that UGLY dress?! It's so DIRTY, you can probably grow fresh mushrooms on it to eat in your salad. Anyway, Victoria says you guys need to sit with US. She wants you to meet our new social media intern, who'll be arriving any minute now. It's actually PERFECT timing!" MacKenzie grinned.

Her nasty little comment about mushrooms was just CRUEL!

I don't even LIKE mushrooms.

We didn't have a choice. So we took a seat at Victoria's table, ordered our ice cream, and tried our best to ignore MacKenzie.

Which, by the way, was IMPOSSIBLE!

Victoria smiled and waved as a person approached our table. "Everyone, meet our NEW social media intern! I think you already know each other . . . !"

ME, IN SHOCK, AND BRANDON,
FREAKING OUT THAT ANDRÉ IS OUR
NEW SOCIAL MEDIA INTERN!

I'll admit, THIS was totally unexpected!

But André is originally from Paris and even has a home here. So it wasn't like he was stalking us or something.

He also speaks fluent French and knows the city really well.

André looked exactly how I remembered him:

1. expensive clothes

2. blinged-out watch

3. tall and lanky

4. a to-die-for smile.

Even though I decided that I am 100% TEAM BRANDON, I can still appreciate why André is SO popular with the girls at my school, especially the CCP girls!

To be honest, I thought André would make a GREAT intern and the PERFECT tour guide for Brandon and me!

Or maybe . . .

NOT!!

Poor Brandon looked like he had just seen a zombie or something. That's when I suddenly remembered that Brandon and André do NOT get along!

At all!

They argue over the SILLIEST things and practically have temper tantrums like they're two spoiled little kids on a playground.

"DUDE! What are YOU doing here?!" Brandon exclaimed, still in shock.

Brandon was completely immune to André's magnetic smile. . . .

WHEN MACKENZIE TOLD ME THE ASSISTANT INTERN POSITION WAS OPEN, I COULDN'T RESIST!

ANDRÉ, THE NEW INTERN!

"Personally, I really WISH you HAD!" Brandon muttered under his breath.

Brandon glared at André. Then he jabbed angrily at

his ice cream like it was trying to crawl out of his bowl and slither away.

"Well, seeing you here is a big surprise!" I said, ignoring Brandon's snarky comment. "So . . . um, how long have you been back in Paris, André?"

"Just a few days. Actually, Nicole, I only came back here to see YOU . . . guys." André smiled and winked.

After what seemed like forever, Victoria announced that she had an interview on a French television show in two hours and needed to get to hair and makeup. Then our meeting was over.

As Brandon and I rode the elevator up to our floor, he seemed unusually quiet and a little . . . tense.

Finally he spoke. "Nikki, I know you and André are good friends, so if you want to spend time with him, that's cool, and I totally get it. However, just because he's YOUR friend doesn't mean he's MINE!"

"Brandon, I'm as surprised as you are that André is here! But he really IS a nice guy once you get to know him."

Brandon definitely wasn't interested in hearing me talk about André. He scrunched up his face like he smelled something unpleasant.

"Well, personally, I don't WANT to get to know him. I'm just sorry things didn't go as planned. We were supposed to hang out, enjoy our gourmet ice cream, and talk. This was just . . . AWFUL!" He sighed.

"It wasn't your fault at all, Brandon. We didn't know Victoria was going to drag us into a meeting. And I LOVED the ice cream! It was . . . DELISH!" I said cheerfully, trying to make him feel better.

"Well, the next time I pick a place for us to hang out, it's going to be MILES away from . . ." He trailed off, staring at the floor.

I couldn't help but wonder how Brandon would have finished his sentence.

Did he want to be miles away from . . .

MacKenzie? Victoria? André?

This very smelly dress that I had to wear AGAIN?!

Brandon was right! Our date WAS a total DISASTER! Even though it wasn't officially a real date.

To cheer him up, I decided to tell him a corny knock-knock joke.

ME: "Knock-knock."

BRANDON (rolling his eyes): "Who's there?"

ME: "Eiffel."

BRANDON: "Eiffel who?"

ME: "Eiffel awful that you feel awful. Get it?"

Brandon smirked. "Yeah, Eiffel Tower. Very funny."

I tried my hardest not to laugh and instead ended up snorting like a pig.

"Now, THAT was actually funny!" Brandon grinned.

By the time we got off the elevator, we were both laughing hysterically.

"So, I'll find a better place for us to hang out and text you, okay?" Brandon smiled.

"I'm already looking forward to it!" I giggled.

Anyway, I think we STILL really enjoyed each other.

Even though things didn't go as planned.

C'est la vie!

☺!

FRIDAY, AUGUST 22

This morning I woke up to an empty suitcase ☹.

Well, almost empty. Brianna's teddy bear, Hans, and her Princess Sugar Plum backpack were still in there HOGGING up most of the space.

I seriously considered tossing both into the Seine River that flows through the heart of Paris. But I'd probably get arrested for dumping garbage into a public waterway and end up missing my flight home.

I was in the hotel lobby staring at the GPS on my phone and trying to figure out where to pick up my clothing order when André walked in through the hotel's front doors.

"*Bonjour, Nicole!*" He smiled. "*What's up?!*"

I was surprised to see him again, until I remembered he's our new assistant intern. He is going to be hanging around quite a bit.

"*Bonjour, André!*" I blushed.

For some strange reason, I always feel SO mature whenever André calls me Nicole.

"Where are you off to this morning?!" he asked.

There was NO WAY I was going to tell him I had arrived in Paris with only a stupid teddy bear and backpack because my bratty little sister had stolen my entire wardrobe.

"Well, it's kind of a long story. I had an . . . issue with my luggage, and now most of my clothing is . . . missing," I explained.

"I'm so sorry to hear that, Nicole. An airline losing your luggage is the WORST! But I'm sure it will turn up. Is there anything I can do to help?!" he asked.

"Actually, yes! I ordered some clothing from a local store, and I just need to go pick it up. Can you tell me the best way to get there?" I asked, showing him the map on my phone. . . .

ANDRÉ AND ME, TRYING TO FIGURE OUT
WHERE THE STORE IS LOCATED

Suddenly André's face lit up.

"I know EXACTLY where this place is! It's my sister's

225

FAVE store. It's only a ten-minute taxi ride. Hey, why don't I just pick up your order for you?!"

"Thanks for the offer, André, but if Victoria has you scheduled to work, I wouldn't want you running errands for me."

The last thing I wanted was for him to get fired on his SECOND day of work for goofing off.

Although now that I think about it, the ONLY thing MacKenzie does is GOOF OFF, but she has NEVER gotten fired.

"Actually, I'm here this morning to have brunch with my godmother. She always complains that I never see her when I'm in the city," he explained.

"OMG! YOU ACTUALLY HAVE BRUNCH WITH YOUR GODMOTHER?! THAT'S ADORABLE AND SO SWEET OF YOU!" I giggled.

André glanced around the lobby to make sure no one overheard me and rolled his eyes.

"Shhh! Let's keep that OUR little secret, okay? Just text me your order info. I'll pick it up and drop it by later," he said, glancing at his watch. "Well, I'd better get going. For every minute I'm late, my godmother makes me spend five minutes listening to boring stories about my childhood."

"She sounds quite charming!" I smiled.

"Actually, she's stubborn and very particular. But she's my godmother, so I've learned to deal with her idiosyncrasies. *Au revoir*, Nicole."

Before I could say good-bye, André smiled, waved, and disappeared into the elevator.

I really appreciated André's offer. But unfortunately it made my life A LOT more complicated.

HOW? His godmother is the MANAGER of our hotel! And apparently she is ALLERGIC to plastic shopping bags! . . .

I was in my room when there was a knock on my door. I assumed it was André returning with my clothing order, but I was WRONG!

IT WAS BRANDON ☺!! SQUEEEEEE!!!

"Hey, Nikki. I found a really cool place for us to hang out. It's two famous fountains called Fontaines de la Concorde. They're really beautiful, and I plan to take some photos. Hopefully, MacKenzie or Victoria won't find us there," he joked.

"Perfect! I'd love to sketch those fountains!" I said. Suddenly I noticed that Brandon was holding a box of chocolates and a mug that said "I LOVE Paris!"

"Oh! I picked these up on the way here!" He smiled shyly. "I hope you like them."

OMG! I could NOT believe Brandon had done that! But I wondered if he was giving them to me as just a good friend or as MORE than a friend.

Suddenly there was ANOTHER knock at the door. . . .

231

One of those bellhop guys pushed a cart into my room that was loaded with beautiful gift boxes.

I could NOT believe that each of my clothing items had been individually gift wrapped and placed in a gorgeous box complete with a bow.

I was VERY impressed!

OMG!

I probably had more presents than the number my entire family got on Christmas Day.

But Brandon was NOT impressed. He seemed to be REALLY irritated.

"NOT AGAIN!" Brandon said, glaring at André. "Dude, WHAT are YOU doing here?! Aren't you supposed to be somewhere else right now? Like in a basement somewhere, working on social media stuff?!"

"YES! I AM doing my JOB!" André shot back. "And right now it's helping Nicole!"

"OKAY, YOU TWO! STOP IT! RIGHT NOW!" I yelled.

Surprised, they both turned and stared at me.

"HE STARTED IT!" they both said,
pointing at each other.

"NO, I DIDN'T!" they both muttered.

I couldn't believe those two were acting like spoiled toddlers. AGAIN! I was NOT their babysitter!

Now that I'd finally gotten my clothing issues sorted out, I was DYING to see the city!

Suddenly my phone dinged. It was a group text message from Victoria.

She said we were having an emergency meeting in her room in ten minutes.

JUST GREAT ☹!!

I turned my attention back to the guys.

"Brandon, thank you so much for the Paris mug and the chocolates. And, André, thank you for your help. But we have a meeting with Victoria in ten minutes, so we'd better get over there!"

Both guys said good-bye and left to get ready for the meeting with Victoria.

Thank goodness I finally had my OWN clothing to wear.

It was probably going to take an hour just to open ALL those boxes.

I was really looking forward to it.

SQUEEEEEEEEEEE ☺!

But the meeting with Victoria, NOT so much!

☹!!

My sketch of a CUTE couple I saw!
#RelationshipGoals

Nicole J. Maxwell

TODAY I VISITED . . .

THE EIFFEL TOWER!

PLACE: The Eiffel Tower
EZ-WAY TO SAY IT: The "EYE-full" Tower
IN FRANCE IT'S CALLED: La Tour Eiffel

FUN FACTS: There are over a hundred antennas on top of the Eiffel Tower that help people in Paris watch TV. Also, three different shades of brown paint make the tower appear even taller than it actually is, with the lightest color at the top and the darkest at the bottom.

WHAT I LIKED BEST!: OMG! The views of the city and different surprises at each of the three levels. To save some time and money AND avoid really long lines, take the stairs to the first two levels. I checked out the glass floor on the first level, then bought homemade ice cream with the money I saved taking the stairs ☺. The staircase to the second level had cool views too! I even saw things I would've missed had I taken the elevators. On the second level I grabbed a few gifts from the souvenir shops, then took a glass-walled elevator to the top level for more breathtaking views!

DON'T MISS!: The dazzling evening light show. Each hour for five minutes, the entire tower sparkles with lights!

Back at L'Hôtel Magnifique de Paris . . .

Nicole J. Maxwell

The Eiffel Tower was first on my list because I'd been admiring it from my hotel window for days.

I saw the cutest couple there that reminded me of Brandon and me. But I think they were probably in college.

I drew a sketch of them taking a selfie together. SQUEEEEEEEEEE ☺!!

I was really looking forward to visiting the Fontaines fountains with Brandon. But he hasn't mentioned it again since that squabble with André.

Actually, he has barely SPOKEN to me since then.

I just hope he isn't mad at me ☹.

Violet said she overheard the guys talking about attending a pro soccer game.

I've barely seen Marc and Theo except at our meetings with Victoria. So Brandon is probably going to be really busy if he's hanging out with them.

I almost forgot a VERY important update! . . .

We received some SHOCKING news at the meeting with Victoria yesterday.

Our photo shoot with *Oh Là Là Chic!* magazine scheduled for Thursday has been put on hold and might be canceled!

Apparently, the photographer is in Milan working with Blaine Blackwell on a major fashion show.

Unless the photographer can finish up in Milan and

fly into Paris by Wednesday evening, our photo shoot is going to be CANCELED.

I'll be disappointed if we aren't able to do the magazine cover. Especially since my bandmates are really looking forward to it.

But MacKenzie will be LIVID! She was planning to use the cover as a way to impress the Bad Boyz with her awesome, um . . . PHOTOGENICITY!

Is that even a word?!

But this ALSO means I WOULDN'T have to explain what happened to my VERY expensive costume that I was supposed to be wearing ON the magazine cover.

And my deep, dark secret would be safe!

I'M SO CONFUSED!

☹!!

OMG! I was SO angry at MacKenzie, I wanted to SCREEEEEEAM ☹!!

Victoria sent MacKenzie and me to pick up complimentary theater tickets for her.

On our way back to the hotel, we saw some young people standing in a long line outside a building with a uniformed attendant monitoring the door.

MacKenzie stopped, stared, and gasped.

"OMG! This is obviously one of those TRENDY French designer POP-UP boutiques! I've read about them in the latest fashion magazines!" she squealed. "Nikki, we need to get in line. HURRY!"

"What's a pop-up boutique?" I asked.

"It's a temporary store that sells designer clothing. But they're only open for a week or two. Sometimes you have to buy a ticket to shop!" . . .

MACKENZIE INSISTS THAT WE VISIT
A FRENCH POP-UP BOUTIQUE

"Some stores only admit people who have a very CHIC vibe. Or as the French say, je ne sais quoi. Like moi!" MacKenzie said, applying her lip gloss.

"It sounds SUPERsnobby, if you ask me," I said.

"Well, no one is asking YOU! And besides, it's NOT snobby. It's just . . . highly EXCLUSIVE! So, Nikki, if they refuse to let you into the building because you're dressed like your grandma, you'll have to just wait outside until I get back, okay?"

News flash! My dress was très chic and brand-new.

Maybe this place WAS one of those pop-up thingies. But personally, I didn't think it was a good idea for us to wander into random buildings just because there was a long line of people waiting to go inside.

MacKenzie purchased two tickets for us. Then we entered a small room that contained a steep, descending spiral staircase. We nervously clutched the handrail as we clambered down five flights. At the bottom was a door that opened into a passageway. . . .

It felt like we were in a dimly lit . . .
UNDERGROUND DUNGEON!

JUST GREAT ☹!

The first thing I noticed was a thick, musty smell. It was also dark, damp, chilly, and very quiet.

Even though we had waited in line with other people, we seemed to be alone.

MacKenzie was a little frazzled but STILL insisted all this was a pop-up shop.

"Nikki, the MOOD is everything! My guess is that they sell a lot of BLACK clothing here!" she said.

We followed the long, dark passageway and continued our descent.

Finally we came to a heavy door. We opened it and entered an underground tunnel. As our eyes slowly adjusted to the dimness, we were NOT prepared for what we saw. . . .

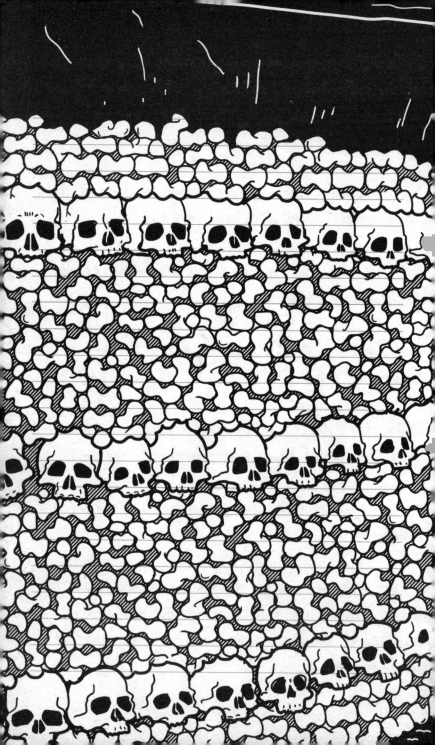

OMG! We were totally surrounded by

HUMAN BONES!!

I didn't want to believe they were REAL!!

Skulls and bones were neatly stacked from floor to ceiling and lined the walls of the corridors.

MacKenzie was FREAKING OUT!

"I d-don't understand!" she stammered. "Where is the designer clothing?! And where are the salespeople?! There's no music or even snacks. This is a really CRUDDY pop-up boutique! I deserve a FULL REFUND!"

MacKenzie and I took a closer look at the wall of skulls and bones. Calling it CREEPY was an understatement. I never saw any sales or management people.

But all the people I DID see were most definitely DEAD!! . . .

249

I couldn't believe what MacKenzie did next. She took out her cell phone along with a brochure she had been given at the door.

"I'm calling management and requesting a full refund," she said as she angrily dialed a number.

She checked her phone battery and tried unsuccessfully to dial a second time. Then she started to panic.

"OMG!! I'M NOT GETTING A CELL PHONE SIGNAL IN HERE!!" she shrieked.

I checked my phone and discovered that I didn't have a signal either.

YIKES ☹!!

WHERE WERE WE?! AND HOW WERE WE GOING TO GET OUT OF HERE?!!

That's when I asked MacKenzie if I could see her brochure. It said . . .

WELCOME TO THE

CATACOMBS OF PARIS!

"THE LABYRINTH OF THE DEAD"

Finally everything made sense.

"Nikki, NOW is NOT the time to catch up
on your reading! We need to get out of here!
This HUMIDITY is MURDERING my hair. I'm going
to try to find a phone signal," MacKenzie yelled.

I began to read the brochure, and OMG! It stated that
this place is basically an underground labyrinth that
contains the REMAINS of more than six million people!

WOW!! That's INCREDIBLE!!

The underground tunnels were originally part of
a series of stone quarries or mines built under
the city of Paris. But when the city's cemeteries
became severely overcrowded and burial space became
scarce, a decision was made in the 1780s to move

251

the remains of dead Parisians to the underground mines, which became known as "ossuaries."

An ossuary is a chest, box, chamber, room, or building serving as the final resting place of HUMAN SKELETAL REMAINS!

I had no idea collecting human bones was a "thing"! But it gets even WEIRDER! . . .

In the early years, the Catacombs were basically just huge piles of random bones. But in 1810 renovations began that transformed the place into a museum of sorts containing "bone-chilling" works of art. It took twelve long years to move all the bodies and bones from the cemeteries of Paris to their current resting place UNDER the city.

The underground corridors are massive, dark, and filled with skeletons. Skulls and femurs are stacked into intricate patterns to create walls of bones.

There are 131 steps down to enter the Catacombs and 112 steps up to exit.

The Catacombs were FASCINATING and definitely more interesting than a pop-up boutique.

Until I realized my LIFE was in danger! It is a famous legend that after MIDNIGHT the walls of the Catacombs CALL to VISITORS, luring them deeper into the tunnels, NEVER to RETURN!

That's when I decided it was time to finish this tour and FAST. Sorry, but I did NOT want to hang around this place any longer! It was time to GO!

I looked for MacKenzie, but she had disappeared into thin air. When I called her name, she didn't answer.

I didn't have a choice but to go deeper into the Catacombs to try to find her.

I felt like I had walked FOREVER when, suddenly, I heard creepy footsteps and raspy breathing.

Getting closer. And closer! And CLOSER! . . .

257

259

OMG! MacKenzie and I pretty much RAN through the rest of the Catacombs. And we didn't stop until we'd climbed the 112 steps up the spiral staircase to get out of there!

When we finally made it back to the street, I was shocked when MacKenzie gave me a big hug.

"Nikki, I know we're FRENEMIES, but thank you for saving my life! We could have been lost in that place FOREVER!! Today I learned two very important things. You are a really NICE person, and THAT was the WORST pop-up shop EVER!"

I was about to tell MacKenzie we had just visited the Paris Catacombs, a popular destination. And we were NEVER actually in any REAL danger. But then I thought . . . NAH! Why bother! I kind of like this NEW MacKenzie.

Maybe I can be friends with THIS girl.

!!

261

ME

TODAY I VISITED . . .
THE LOUVRE MUSEUM!

PLACE: The Louvre Museum
EZ-WAY TO SAY IT: The "Loov-ruh" Museum
IN FRANCE IT'S CALLED: Musée du Louvre

SHORT HISTORY: The Louvre Museum is the BIGGEST
and the most-visited art museum in the entire WORLD!

FUN FACTS: The museum is so GINORMOUS that it's
humanly IMPOSSIBLE for you to see the 35,000
pieces in one day. Even if I spent ONLY thirty
seconds looking at EACH item for twenty-four hours
straight (with NO bathroom and eating breaks), it
would STILL take TWELVE WHOLE DAYS for me
to see everything! And that's EXCLUDING the other
345,000 pieces of art that are NOT even out for
display at the museum. To see ALL the collections at
the museum, you would literally have to LIVE there for
over four months, which could be a bit EXHAUSTING!

WHAT I LIKED BEST!: My FAVE exhibits were the
Egyptian sphinx and the Nike of Samothrace, a two-
thousand-year-old, eighteen-foot-tall Greek goddess
with wings carved out of marble. She's missing feet,
arms, and a head (yes, that's A LOT of body parts!!),

263

but she's still beautiful and powerful, and just looks SO majestic! #Iwokeuplikethis ☺! Now I understand why Nike shoes are named after this Greek goddess of victory!

For a snack I grabbed a double chocolaty chip crème Frappuccino from Starbucks. Yes! There's actually a Starbucks in the Louvre Museum, under the pyramid. I also had a warm, deliciously gooey chocolate croissant from a nearby popular French gourmet bakery! Definitely . . . OOH LA LA!

DON'T MISS!: You MUST see Leonardo da Vinci's _Mona Lisa_, which is the museum's most popular exhibit! The painting has its own bodyguards and a private mailbox because of all the love letters it receives. OMG! Mona actually gets LOVE letters?! I'm so JELLY! To see the painting (which is behind bulletproof glass), you can either wait in a SUPERlong TSA-looking zigzag line or take a pic from the back of the room.

FINAL THOUGHTS: I LOVED finally seeing this ICONIC masterpiece in spite of her slightly creepy smile. Like most people, I was surprised that it's so small, only 21 × 30 inches, since Mona's worldwide rep is HUMONGOUS!

TUESDAY, AUGUST 26

OMG! We just got a group text from Victoria that the magazine photo shoot is definitely still on and scheduled for Thursday! JUST GREAT ☹!!

This means I have less than forty-eight hours to find a new dress similar in color and style to the one Blaine designed for me.

But that's not all. It ALSO needs to match my bandmates.

"I don't mean to be negative, but what's the likelihood we're actually going to find THIS dress?!" I sighed. "Maybe I should just come clean and tell Victoria what happened."

"So YOUR idea is to tell Victoria you threw away a $5,000 custom designer dress because you were having a bad day!" Chloe said, rolling her eyes.

"She'll probably FIRE you on the spot AND make you PAY for the dress!" Zoey grumbled.

"OMG! I hadn't thought of that!" I groaned, feeling even MORE hopeless.

"To be honest, it shouldn't be too difficult to find a similar dress. We ARE in the fashion capital of the WORLD, right?!" Zoey reasoned. "This is the BEST place on EARTH to look for a dress!"

No question about it! My BFF Zoey is a GENIUS!

So we called area dress shops to ask if they had any gold dresses similar to a Blaine Blackwell. Several had REAL Blaine Blackwells, but they started at €3,000. That's euros! And YES! Those dresses practically cost MORE than our family CAR!

After almost two hours, we finally found a shop with a gold dress that might work! It was €300 and on sale for 25% off. They placed the dress on hold so we could come and see it.

Chloe, Zoey, and I took a taxi to a quaint little boutique fifteen minutes from our hotel. The dresses there were absolutely GORGEOUS!

We couldn't resist doing a TRY-ON-A-THON!
Complete with shoes and accessories. . . .

Nicole J. Maxwell

CHLOE

Nicole J. Maxwell

ZOEY

Nicole J. Maxwell

269

NIKKI

Nicole J. Maxwell

OMG! We all agreed that MY dress was PERFECT!

For a cheap knockoff of a Blaine Blackwell, anyway.

It was the exact same color gold and even had a jeweled bodice.

"I'll TAKE IT!" I said happily to the salesclerk.

Chloe, Zoey, and I did a group hug! I couldn't believe I was going to be able to do the magazine photo shoot after all.

"What a beautiful dress!" The salesclerk smiled. "We can barely keep this style in stock. And since we're having a sale today, this €400 dress at 25% off is €300 plus tax, for a total of €360. Will that be cash or credit?"

Chloe, Zoey, and I exchanged worried glances. We thought the dress was €300 minus 25% off plus tax for a total of €270. So we'd managed to scrounge up €270 between us with our stipend money. But we were €90 short! My heart sank.

We were panicking when the front door opened and
we heard a very familiar voice. . . .

Nicole J. Maxwell

IT WAS MACKENZIE!

Worst timing ever!

The salesclerk cleared her throat and asked again, "So, girls, will that be cash or credit card?"

"Actually, we're trying to decide that right now," Zoey answered, tapping her chin. "Do we want to use cash or our credit card? Hmm . . . ," she stalled.

"Hey, I have an idea!" Chloe said. "Let's just borrow €90 from . . . OW!! That HURT!"

I had just given Chloe a swift kick, and Zoey shot her a dirty look.

MacKenzie narrowed her eyes at Chloe. "Are you asking ME to loan you €90?"

"Well, I, um . . . ," Chloe stammered as she glanced at Zoey and me.

MacKenzie smiled. "Chloe, of course I'll loan you €90. So, what are you buying?"

"Actually, it's a dress for . . ."

"ME!" Zoey interrupted. "Chloe wants to buy a
DRESS for ME! Tomorrow is my . . . BIRTHDAY!
And we're . . . I mean . . . SHE is €90 short."

Chloe stared at Zoey. "What?! I thought your
birthday was . . . OW!!" Chloe whined again.

"We'd like to pay for the dress with cash," Zoey
told the salesclerk.

"What a gorgeous dress!" MacKenzie gushed as we
placed our money on the counter.

She opened her purse and peered inside. "I'm really
sorry! I thought I had €90, but I don't."

My heart dropped ☹! AGAIN!

"So I'll just put the dress on my credit card,"
MacKenzie said. "Chloe, you can pay me back after
we get home from Paris. How does THAT sound?"

To be honest, it sounded TOO good to be TRUE!
MacKenzie paid for the dress with her credit card. . . .

ME, SHOCKED AND SURPRISED THAT
MACKENZIE IS BEING SO NICE!

"Can we have the dress steamed and delivered to our hotel?" MacKenzie asked the salesclerk.

"Definitely. And delivery is free," the salesclerk answered. "We'll leave the dress with the front desk tomorrow afternoon."

OMG! I was LOVING this NEW MacKenzie.

I should have SAVED her LIFE months ago!

☺!!

Nicole J. Maxwell

ME

TODAY I VISITED . . .

THE ARC DE TRIOMPHE!

PLACE: The Arc de Triomphe
EZ-WAY TO SAY IT: The "Ark duh tree-awnf"
IN FRANCE IT'S CALLED: Arc de Triomphe
de l'Étoile (duh ley-twal)

SHORT HISTORY: This took thirty years to build! It includes beautiful sculptures, inscriptions, the names of 660 officers, important treaties, and scenes from Napoleon's military victories all intricately carved into the limestone.

FUN FACTS: It's located in the center of one of the busiest intersections in Paris. Twelve different streets come together to form a CHAOTIC roundabout with literally no lanes, sidewalks, or even stop signs! From above, the arch looks like it's the center of a star (étoile) with streets shooting out like rays of light.

WHAT I LIKED BEST!: Views! Views! And more views! By walking up the Champs-Élysées (although I personally rode a hot-pink moped there), you'll get a full view of the arch and see just how majestic it looks sitting at the top of the hill. I had breathtaking views of the ENTIRE city plus a bunch of famous landmarks! And I was actually able to see the Eiffel Tower light show.

Nicole J. Maxwell

When I arrived back at the hotel from the Arc de Triomphe, Chloe and Zoey were in the lobby waiting for MacKenzie. The dress had already been delivered, and the three of them had agreed to pick it up from the front desk.

I had to admit, I felt SUPERnervous. WHY?!

Because I was PRETENDING that it WASN'T my dress. Chloe was PRETENDING that SHE was buying the dress as a birthday gift for Zoey. And Zoey was PRETENDING that today was her birthday and the dress was a gift from Chloe.

279

That said, we PROBABLY should have come up with a strategy that didn't involve a PACK OF LIES!! I mean, WHO did we think we were? MACKENZIE HOLLISTER?!

I spotted MacKenzie at the front desk, and we anxiously scrambled after her. By the time we caught up with her, she had already picked up the dress and was admiring it intently.

"I knew this gorgeous dress looked familiar!" MacKenzie exclaimed. "It's a knockoff of the design that Blaine Blackwell did for your band!"

Chloe, Zoey, and I just stared at her and shrugged.

"Well, that's strange! Why would you want a knockoff so desperately that you'd borrow money to buy it?" MacKenzie asked, eyeballing us suspiciously like we'd just robbed a bank or something.

"Sorry, MacKenzie, we'd love to stay and chat with you, but we'll just take Zoey's dress and get going!" Chloe said as she SNATCHED the dress from her. . . .

SNATCH!!

CHLOE

MacKenzie yanked the dress from Chloe and yelled,
"Sorry! But it's MY dress! I paid for
it with MY credit card!"

Then Zoey grabbed the dress from MacKenzie and said, "It's MY birthday present from Chloe! So the dress belongs to ME!"

MacKenzie snatched the dress from Zoey and screeched, "You already have a real Blaine Blackwell, so this knockoff IS MINE!!"

People in the lobby were starting to stare at us!

It was KA-RAY-ZEE because my BFFs and I were literally having a tug-of-war over the dress with MacKenzie.

She was pulling on the dress with all her might while my BFFs and I were doing the same thing.

"LET GO! IT'S MINE!!" the four of us yelled.

Suddenly we heard a loud . . .

R–R–R–I–I–I–P!!

All four of us just stared at the dress in shock like . . .

OOPS 😦!!

Finally, MacKenzie grabbed the dress and snarled, "This dress is MINE! And NO ONE is going to take it from me!!"

ME, HAVING A TOTAL MELTDOWN OVER THE DAMAGED DRESS DRAMA

OMG! I could NOT believe this was actually happening to me!

My BFFs and I spent hours searching dozens of stores and had FINALLY found the perfect dress!

And now it was basically in SHREDS!!

That's when we decided to just let MacKenzie KEEP the STUPID DRESS!!

Chloe, Zoey, and I trudged back to our rooms feeling totally defeated.

"Nikki, I'm really sorry things turned out so badly!" Zoey sniffed.

"What are you going to do now?" Chloe asked.

I sighed deeply and bit my lip to keep from crying. "Well, the LAST thing I want to do is show up at the photo shoot NOT wearing my designer dress. I'm sure that will only make things WORSE! Victoria will probably FIRE me on the spot and make me

SWIM back home! So I'll call Trevor tomorrow and explain everything and offer to pay for the dress."

"WOW! That's A LOT of babysitting money!" Chloe exclaimed.

I hugged my BFFs, wished them good luck at the photo shoot tomorrow, and closed my door.

I traveled halfway around the world to Paris with my bandmates just to do that photo shoot for the *Oh Là Là Chic!* magazine cover!

But now that DREAM has turned into a NIGHTMARE!

I collapsed on my bed in tears.

MacKenzie has WON!!

☹!!

I barely got any sleep last night. Since I was wide awake, I texted Victoria at 7:00 a.m. to let her know I was SICK and wouldn't be able to do the photo shoot.

I told her I had suddenly started to feel VERY nauseous.

I was actually telling the truth about that part.

I was SO sick of my CRAPPY life, I wanted to . . . VOMIT ☹!!

Victoria was surprisingly sympathetic. She told me to get some rest, and if I was feeling better before they left at 9:30 a.m., I could join them. She said not to worry, that MacKenzie could take my place.

I was SO angry that MacKenzie had selfishly kept my dress and then destroyed it! WHY did I trust that rattlesnake in glitter lip gloss to begin with?!

Today she was going to have MY spot on the cover of *Oh Là Là Chic!* magazine.

Just like she had planned all along.

I felt totally helpless.

I had been away from home for ten days and was starting to feel homesick.

When I opened my suitcase and saw Brianna's stupid teddy bear, Hans, I suddenly realized how much I was missing my family!

Even Brianna.

To make matters worse, I hadn't seen Brandon since last Friday, and I missed him, too. I wonder if he is mad at me.

Right then I felt so frustrated and alone that I took Hans out of Brianna's Princess Sugar Plum backpack and gave him a BIG HUG. . . .

HANS STILL SMELLED A LITTLE LIKE
DIRTY GYM SOCKS, BUT I DIDN'T EVEN CARE!

I was about to put Hans back inside the backpack
when I noticed there was something rolled up and
tucked into the bottom of it.

I grabbed at a bundle of fabric and pulled . . .

It looked vaguely familiar. But I wasn't sure. Until I reached in and gathered it all into my arms.

OMG! I COULD NOT BELIEVE MY EYES!

BRIANNA HAD STUFFED MY COSTUME
INTO THE BOTTOM OF HER BACKPACK!

The Amazing Brianna-dini really could make things
reappear! Even my SHOES were inside! She must
have taken my costume out of the garbage bin right
after I had thrown it away.

Brianna had also written me the sweetest note:

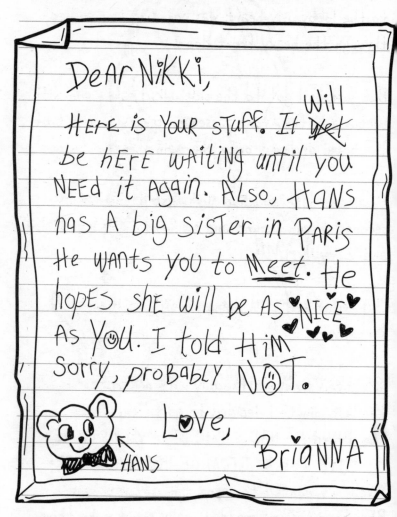

DeAr NiKKi,

HErE is YOUR STUFF. It Will ~~Wet~~ be hErE wAiTiNg until you NEED it AgAin. ALSo, HANS has A big SiSTer in PARiS He WANTS YOU to Meet. He hopES SHE will be AS NICE AS YOU. I told HiM Sorry, proBAbLY NOT.

Love,

BriANNA

HANS

Suddenly I had the CRAZIEST idea! It was 9:15 a.m., and our van was scheduled to leave for the magazine office at 9:30 a.m.

I got dressed as fast as I could and raced down to the lobby. My heart was pounding as I pushed through the heavy front doors.

But just as I got to the sidewalk, I saw a van with Victoria in the front passenger seat pulling out of the hotel driveway onto the main street.

I was too late and had just missed the van by seconds! I spun around and slammed right into Chloe and Zoey. BAM!!

"Wh—what are YOU doing here?!" we stammered to each other.

"I wanted to spend the day with my BFFs. So at the last minute I decided to go to the photo shoot," I explained.

"Well, we wanted to spend the day with our BFF . . . ," Zoey began.

"So at the last minute we decided NOT to go to the photo shoot," Chloe finished.

Suddenly they noticed what I was wearing.

"OMG, NIKKI! YOU FOUND YOUR COSTUME!!" they both exclaimed. "WHERE?!"

"I'll explain all of that later," I said. "But right now we need to get to that magazine cover photo shoot!"

While Zoey was busy looking up the address of the magazine office, Chloe and I were trying to figure out the best way to get there.

We had no idea how to take the subway or the bus systems, and we didn't have time to find a taxi or rideshare driver who spoke English.

We looked around the busy street in frustration. In the park next door we noticed teens laughing and enjoying the sunny day.

Chloe, Zoey, and I came up with a BRILLIANT idea at the same time. . . .

CHLOE, ZOEY, AND ME, ON OUR WAY TO THE
MAGAZINE PHOTO SHOOT!

Luckily, we made it there. ALIVE!!

The photo shoot was a huge success!

And so was our magazine cover! SQUEEE ☺!

During the entire photo shoot, MacKenzie was GLARING at me like an ANGRY TROLL.

And after we finished, she gave me the dirtiest look and rolled her EYES so hard I thought they were going to POP OUT of their sockets and be mistaken by a Parisian for the French delicacy ESCARGOTS (snails slathered in butter and garlic)!

MacKenzie actually wore that ripped dress as a two-piece ensemble. I think she was going for "SHABBY CHIC." But the dress was a total fashion disaster that looked more like "TRENDY TRASH."

My bandmates and I agreed that this trip was the most AWESOME Savage Summer Challenge EVER!

Maybe next year we can do something even more KA-RAY-ZEE, like walk the runway for PARIS FASHION WEEK!

Hey, a girl can DREAM.

SQUEEEEEEEEEE! ☺!

FRIDAY, AUGUST 29

OMG! I couldn't believe I was standing outside one of the oldest and most famous ART STORES in the world....

Nicole J. Maxwell

SENNELIER! SQUEEEEEEE ☺!

The most AMAZING thing about this place is that it has created paints and provided supplies for some of the world's GREATEST artists, including Degas, Cézanne, Picasso, and Van Gogh.

And, of course, NOW I can add MY name . . .

Nicole J. Maxwell

to the list of inspired artists who have passed through its doors ☺.

Sennelier is most famous for its large assortment of paint and will even create special colors that are requested by artists. How about Lip Gloss Pink?

Nicole J. Maxwell

The store was so fascinating, I could have just wandered around looking at art supplies for hours!

However, today I was shopping for a professional set of artists' COLORED PENCILS. . . .

Nicole J. Maxwell

And it was my LUCKY DAY because they were a WHOPPING 50% off! SQUEEEEEEEE ☺!

I paid for the pencils and took one last look around the WONDERFUL store!

Nicole J. Maxwell

I couldn't wait to get my colored pencils back to my hotel room!

At first I wondered what projects I could use them for. Then I got the BEST idea EVER!! . . .

Nicole J. Maxwell

I have an endless supply of my very OWN artwork to color right inside my DIARY!! SQUEEEEE ☺!

SATURDAY, AUGUST 30

It was hard to believe we had been in Paris twelve whole days.

It still felt like we'd just arrived.

My bandmates and I were packed up and on our way to Charles de Gaulle Airport for our flight back home.

Thank goodness things went a lot smoother on our trip home.

Chloe, Zoey, and I even had time to visit a gift store and shop for souvenirs for family and friends.

While my BFFs admired hats and T-shirts, I found the most ADORABLE teddy bear.

Not only did I successfully help Hans find his BIG SISTER in Paris, but Brianna was WRONG!

She WAS just as NICE as ME ☺! . . .

Nicole J. Maxwell

I was really looking forward to Brandon and me sitting next to each other in first class on the flight home.

I thought we'd spend the entire trip laughing and talking about how much fun we'd had in Paris and what a beautiful city it is. But Brandon was quiet and seemed kind of down.

Chloe and Zoey noticed it too, because they were whispering about it. Very loudly.

I overheard them say, "This is really BAD! Nikki and Brandon aren't even TALKING to each other!"

That's when I totally lost it and yelled, "CHLOE AND ZOEY, PLEASE SHUT UP! Brandon and I can HEAR every single WORD you're saying!"

But I just said it inside my head, so no one else heard it but me.

Brandon was staring out the window when I took a deep breath, tapped his shoulder, and said . . .

"Yeah, me too," he agreed. "Nikki, I just want you to be happy! And if you're interested in André, I understand. I don't know how serious you are about him, but he's obviously very serious about YOU."

"Brandon, André and I are just friends. That's it."

"But what about all that 'mon amour' stuff? I'm fluent in French, and I heard you calling each other 'my love.' And the cartload of gifts! That looks SERIOUS to me! Do you have ANY idea how much all that stuff cost?!" Brandon sighed.

"Actually, I know EXACTLY how much all that cost, because my MOTHER purchased it with HER debit card. From a store called Mon Amour. Brianna swiped all my clothes, so I arrived in Paris with just pajamas, socks, and bunny slippers. André picked up my order from the store, and his godmother wrapped everything."

Brandon stared at me, confused. "Mon Amour is a . . . STORE?! Seriously? But I thought . . . ! I guess I assumed a lot of things, but I was wrong. I had no idea you were having issues." And then he said . . .

I must admit, I was a little surprised when Brandon apologized. But I was glad he did. He also said he was going to try harder to get along with André. Even when he called me Nicole.

I couldn't help but giggle at Brandon thinking André and I were calling each other 'my love' every time we'd mentioned the store Mon Amour. Which was probably at least a DOZEN times.

I was also happy Brandon said he wanted to be a "great friend." But I couldn't help but wonder if he meant JUST a great friend or MORE than a great friend. I need to ask my BFFs about that.

Brandon brushed his bangs out of his eyes and gave me a HUGE smile. I didn't know if I had butterflies in my stomach or our plane was falling out of the sky. But I felt like . . . WHEEEEEEEE ☺!

"Well, Nikki, at least we get to sit together on the long trip HOME. Personally, I think it's going to be the BEST part of the trip!" Brandon joked as he grabbed his cell phone to take a selfie of us. . . .

Suddenly I remembered that cute couple I saw at the Eiffel Tower. They took a selfie just like Brandon and I did.

But my GOOFY BFFs, CHLOE and ZOEY, didn't

PHOTOBOMB

THEIR selfie like they did OURS!! . . .

Sacrebleu!

☺!!

SUNDAY, AUGUST 31

Au revoir, Paris!

We arrived back home yesterday!

J'adore Paris! It was beautiful, magnificent, classy, and everything I dreamed it would be.

I LOVED staying at one of the finest luxury hotels and seeing all the fascinating sights.

But it was WONDERFUL to be home again.

Nothing makes me feel quite as SECURE as being with the people I LOVE most . . .

MY FAMILY ☺!

I couldn't wait to CHILLAX in my very own comfy bedroom again. Even though it's NOT a fancy five-star accommodation with room service and housekeepers. . . .

Nicole J. Maxwell

Paris Fashion Illustrations

. . . IT'S MINE! SQUEEEEEEE ☺!!

I learned a valuable life lesson on this Paris adventure: NEVER give up on your DREAMS!

But I learned the MOST from my bratty sister, Brianna: NEVER, EVER stop believing in MAGIC! . . .

NIKKI, I'M SO HAPPY YOU'RE BACK HOME! I REALLY MISSED YOU!

I gave Brianna a big hug and a teddy bear that was really from Paris: Hans's older sister, HANNAH ☺!

Brandon came by to share the photos he took while we were in Paris. . . .

BRANDON AND ME, HANGING OUT,
ADMIRING PHOTOS OF PARIS

He's a SUPERtalented photographer and a really great friend.

However, my BEST memories of Brandon are the ones stored in my HEART.

NOT on my cell phone.

Excusez—moi.

C'est la vie.

I'm SUCH a DORK!!

☺!!

NIKKI'S GUIDE TO
FRENCH WORDS AND TERMS

PAGE	FRENCH	ENGLISH
61	OOH LA LA!!! J'ai vraiment besoin de commencer à pratiquer mon français!	OMG!!! I really need to start practicing my French!
61	très chic	very stylish
162	OOH LA LA!	OMG!
162	TRÈS CHIC	VERY STYLISH
178	BONJOUR, PARIS!	HELLO, PARIS!
178	Je m'appelle Nikki!	My name is Nikki!
178	J'adore Paris!	I love Paris!
185	Excusez—moi	Excuse me
187	TRÈS MAGNIFIQUE!	VERY MAGNIFICENT!
189	Mon Amour	My Love
191	J'adore Paris	I love Paris
192	Oh Là Là Chic!	OMG Chic!
195	Non, merci. Je reviens tout de suite.	No, thank you. I'll be right back.
196	très chic!	very stylish!
197	Je voudrais que vous sentiez mes pieds.	I'd like you to smell my feet.

PAGE	FRENCH	ENGLISH
198	JE VOUDRAIS QUE VOUS SENTIEZ MES PIEDS!	I'D LIKE YOU TO SMELL MY FEET!
200	Oh là là là là là!!	OMG!!
200	T'ES GROSSIÈRE, MÉCHANTE!	YOU ARE RUDE, NASTY GIRL!
201	ALLEZ-VOUS-EN!!	GO AWAY!!
202	Je voudrais que vous sentiez mes pieds.	I'd like you to smell my feet.
208	MOI!!	ME!!
212	maître d'	head waiter at a restaurant, in French called maître d'hôtel
213	S'IL VOUS PLAÎT!	PLEASE!
222	C'est la vie!	That's life!
223	Bonjour	Hello
224	Bonjour	Hello
227	Au revoir	Good-bye
231	MON AMOUR	MY LOVE
239	Oh Là Là Chic!	OMG Chic!
243	je ne sais quoi	I don't know what, or a great quality that can't be described
243	moi	me
243	très chic	very stylish

PAGE	FRENCH	ENGLISH
264	OOH LA LA!	OMG!
278	étoile	star
286	Oh Là Là Chic!	OMG Chic!
298	Oh Là Là Chic!	OMG Chic!
299	ESCARGOTS	SNAILS
302	crayons de couleur	colored pencils
302	EN SOLDES 50% DE RÉDUCTION	ON SALE 50% OFF
304	crayons de couleur	colored pencils
306	souvenirs	souvenirs
306	Très Chic	Very Stylish
306	L'amour	Love
307	J'ADORE PARIS	I LOVE PARIS
307	Cartes postales	Postcards
307	Bonjour	Hello
310	mon amour	my love
310	Mon Amour	My Love
314	Sacrebleu!	Oh my gosh!
315	Au revoir, Paris!	Good-bye, Paris!
315	J'adore Paris!	I love Paris!
319	Excusez-moi	Excuse me
319	C'est la vie	That's life

ACKNOWLEDGMENTS

SQUEEEE!!!! We've just finished Dork Diaries Book 15, thanks to my talented and dedicated Team Dork!

A special thanks to my WONDERFUL Senior Vice President, Valerie Garfield. Thank you for your steadfast support and for immersing yourself into Nikki Maxwell's world so quickly and graciously. Your kindness, enthusiasm, and witty humor never fail to brighten our day! I look forward to working with you to introduce a new generation of ADORKABLE fans to Nikki's COLORFUL life!

To Karin Paprocki, my TALENTED Executive Art Director. You continue to amaze me with your creativity and ability to magically oversee such things as page layout and artwork placement at the speed of light. Thank you for your awesome vision and design expertise!

To Katherine Devendorf, my AMAZING Vice President, Managing Editorial Director. Thank you for copyediting my book with your incredible skill and precision. You make a difficult task seem so easy!

To Daniel Lazar, my PHENOMENAL agent at Writers House. Thanks for your friendship, patience, and brutal honesty, and for knowing when to wear your baseball cap. Despite our crazy roller-coaster ride these past few years, I can honestly say that I still enjoy Zoom calls and pineapples. And I'm SUPERexcited for our next chapter. You're the best agent EVER!

To my INCREDIBLE Team Dork at Aladdin/Simon & Schuster, Jon Anderson, Julie Doebler, Anna Jarzab, Caitlin Sweeny, Alissa Nigro, Lisa Moraleda, Chrissy Noh, Nicole Russo, Ashley Mitchell, Nadia Almahdi, Jenn Rothkin, Ian Reilly, Christina Solazzo, Nicole Tai, Lauren Forte, Rebecca Vitkus, Chel Morgan, Crystal Velasquez, Jon Howard, Stephanie Voros, Amy Habayeb, Michelle Leo, Amy Beaudoin, Christina Pecorale, Gary Urda, and the entire sales force. Thanks for your continued commitment, support, and hard work!

A special thanks to my REMARKABLE Writers House assistant, Torie Doherty-Munro, and my Writers House foreign rights agents, Cecilia de la Campa and Alessandra Birch, for helping Dork Diaries become an international bestseller. Your efforts do not go unnoticed!

And to Deena, Zoé, Marie, Jessica, Bree, Cori, Presli, Dolly Ann, and Franklene, thanks for everything you do!

A special thanks to Sophie Sennelier, the owner of Sennelier art store, who so graciously allowed Nikki Maxwell to visit her wonderful shop and share the experience with our readers around the world.

To my SPECTACULAR daughter and GIFTED illustrator, Nikki, thanks for your brilliant artistry, late nights, and love. I couldn't ask for a better daughter. To my sister Kim, my champion and cheerleader for all things DORKY. Thanks for being a forever fan and advocate. I'd also like to acknowledge with gratitude the love and unwavering support of my entire family!

And last but not least, to my Dork Diaries superfans! Thanks for loving my book series and for selecting the perfect Parisian cover of chic checks. Always remember to let your inner DORK shine through! ☺

Rachel Renée Russell is the #1

New York Times bestselling author of the blockbuster book series Dork Diaries and the bestselling series The Misadventures of Max Crumbly.

There are more than fifty-five million copies of her books in print worldwide, and they have been translated into thirty-seven languages.

She enjoys working with her daughter Nikki, who helps illustrate her books.

Rachel's message is "Always let your inner dork shine through!"